BETRAYED

WOLF GATHERINGS, BOOK SIX

BECCA JAMESON

Copyright © 2014 by Becca Jameson

All characters and events in this book are fictitious. And resemblance to actual persons living or dead is strictly coincidental.

All rights reserved.

No part of this book may be reproduced in any form or by any electronic or mechanical means, including information storage and retrieval systems, without written permission from the author, except for the use of brief quotations in a book review.

❀ Created with Vellum

ACKNOWLEDGMENTS

To my editor, Lisa Dugan, who slapped me silly pointing out the "plot holes you could drive a pickup truck through" on this one. The rewriting was arduous, but the finished product is much better as a result of her input and countless hours of brainstorming!

CHAPTER 1

"I don't like it, Dad. He's my only child."

Shit. Marcus had stepped onto his parents' front porch seconds before he heard his mother's voice. Just his luck it was warm enough out today to leave the front door open and let the breeze blow in through the screen door.

And thank God, because the last person on earth Marcus wanted to face was dear old Granddad, Melvin Cunningham.

"That's entirely the point, Lora. You're *my* only child also. Which makes Marcus the only person alive capable of carrying on the family genes."

Marcus cringed. He hated the way his grandfather spoke to his mother. He'd never treated her like an adult. And keeping with tradition, his father treated her no differently.

As if on cue, his father spoke next. "Listen to him, Lora. He knows what he's talking about."

Great. They were all gathered in the living room

discussing his future, or what they expected to make of it, without his input. Figured.

His grandfather cleared his throat and continued. "Carl's right. Things have changed. Medical research has made drastic improvements in the last two years. My people have isolated specific chromosomes that make up our DNA and give us the ability to shift. Do you know what that means?"

His mother must have shaken her head because he didn't hear anything from her before his grandfather continued. He could picture her staring wearily at her father. He'd seen the look many times. It hadn't done him any good growing up, however. She'd never had the balls to actually stand up for Marcus and keep his father and grandfather from tampering with him.

As a kid he'd spent summers at military camps with other shifters. His grandfather had encouraged his mother to "toughen him up."

In his late teens he'd felt like a guinea pig when his grandfather had shown up with a vial of some horrific substance he insisted would make Marcus stronger. "You're far too scrawny," he said. "This will beef you up, boy."

Marcus hated the drug and the subsequent series of medicines he'd been given over the next several years. Nothing had made him stronger except time. The pile of drugs had only altered his state of mind and infuriated him.

"It means we're on the cusp of a breakthrough. It means everything to our species, Lora."

"What do you have in mind, Dad?" Marcus's father

spoke now. He'd never had a good relationship with his own father and called Marcus's grandfather Dad for as long as Marcus could remember.

"I'll need to bring him in to our facility in Minnesota. After a bit of testing, he should easily be a candidate for gene therapy."

"Dad, he's a grown man. Twenty-six years old," his mother protested. "You can't haul him off to Minnesota for medical research. He'd never agree to it."

"He doesn't have to, Lora. No one mentioned anything about agreement." His father's voice was cold. Calculated.

Marcus cringed. *They have to be kidding.*

He'd known his parents were involved in something less than stellar for a long time, but he'd never expected this.

His mother was right. He was no child now. He was a grown man. He'd been significantly shaped by his strange childhood. Even though he'd been small as a boy, he learned to fight. He learned to use weapons. He took what he learned at military camp and applied it in positive ways. He was never what his grandfather had hoped, but he became a stronger, more self-sufficient adult as a result of his training.

"The drugs you gave him over a year ago didn't work correctly. You said so yourself. And you nearly caused us undue embarrassment at The Gathering by encouraging him to mate with more than one woman. I don't know how we will be able to show our faces at the next Gathering. The Davises must be furious," his mother said.

His father fielded that one. "Lora, nobody cares about the damn Gathering."

"Those are our friends, Carl. The people we've enjoyed the company of our entire adult lives."

"Those relationships are trite, Lora," his grandfather said. "I don't give a shit about those pansy-assed, lower-class shifters."

His mother gasped so loud, Marcus could hear her. He held his breath, not daring to move a muscle.

His stomach clenched thinking about Kathleen and Mackenzie Davis, the two sisters his grandfather encouraged him to mate with at The Gathering last year. Every day he struggled to block the weekend out of his mind.

"Listen to me, Lora." Granddad's voice rose. "Those damn gatherings are over. We're about to go to war. Don't you realize that?"

"Why would we do that? Against whom?"

"It's a wolf-eat-wolf world now, girl. Survival of the fittest. Last week those bastards snatched twelve women from their mates and stole them away to the Spencer Ranch in Texas. Did you know that? Our people must mobilize."

"What are you talking about? 'Our people.' What does that mean? We're all shifters. There isn't a *them* and an *us*."

"There is now," his father said. "And we're going to be on the winning side of this battle, Lora. I intend to fight for our survival as a species. I have to agree with your father. And Marcus needs to man up and do his duty for our side. If those bastards want a war, they'll have it."

"What bastards? Who are you talking about?" she asked.

His grandfather cackled maniacally. "Anyone working for The Head Council." The man sounded exasperated. "Listen to your husband, Lora. This is war. Marcus is strong. He works in construction. He's an asset to our team. Even with his limited military experience, he's got what it takes now that he's fully grown. I need him."

Military? Even after ten summers at military camp, Marcus had never considered joining any armed forces. The primary branch of military for shifters was called NAR, North American Reserves. They were under the jurisdiction of The Head Council. However, except for occasionally hearing about the organization, Marcus knew very little about them. They weren't the group he'd trained under. The camps Marcus had been sent to as a child had been private.

And he could see why now. Apparently his grandfather and his father were opposed to The Head Council. No wonder some of the tactics he'd learned at those military camps had seemed excessive.

Had his grandfather been grooming him all those years? Had he been training with a secret subversive force?

Marcus closed his eyes. He felt sick to his stomach.

His mother gasped. "Just because he's strong doesn't mean you have the right to shuffle him off to some medical facility for experimental drug treatment."

"It means exactly that. After he got out of his teens, when I thought he'd end up scrawny and weak, he's made up for it in spades in recent years. Precisely the sort of man we need on our team."

Marcus cringed again at his grandfather's insistence. The last thing he wanted to do was join dear old Granddad at some strange medical facility in Minnesota.

With the exception of the nasty interlude at The Gathering last spring, he'd been living his own life for over six years. It had taken him a while as a teenager to realize he didn't want to take anything his parents or grandfather prescribed, but eventually he'd started hiding the pills anywhere he could and pretending to do as they requested.

Instead of bulking up with drugs, he'd worked out. Hard. The physique he had today was thanks to his own hard labor, not some steroid or mind-altering drug.

The Gathering had been an exception out of his control. His grandfather had cornered him and jabbed a needle into his thigh before he could protest. The entire weekend had been a series of stupid actions while he'd been under the suggestive drugged state. He'd been horny as hell, his cock rigid for forty-eight hours. So when Granddad pointed out first one woman and then another as his mate, he'd easily succumbed to temptation.

He'd known something was off, but he'd been helpless to stop the madness. And two sisters had suffered under his ruthless insistence. Nothing could erase the memory and the guilt. Since that weekend, he hadn't dated anyone, human or shifter.

He forced himself to concentrate on his grandfather's words instead of lamenting the past. "Get in the game, Lora. You're either with us or you're against us. Those damn law-abiding rule followers are in for a rude awakening when they find out what we're capable of. We hadn't intended to mobilize so quickly, but the Romulus is ready. And we've been backed up against a wall with this mass kidnapping."

Who the fuck is the Romulus? He'd never heard of them.

"Are you trying to tell me the Spencers actually kidnapped a dozen women against their will? I can't believe that. I've known Natalie and Jerome for years. They're the kindest people I've ever met." His mother's voice faded as she spoke. She must have turned away or lowered her voice.

"That's exactly what I'm saying. Well, not the Spencers themselves. They're just harboring the women. But we're moving in and will beat them at their own game in no time."

"You intend to fight them? On their property?" Her voice trembled.

"Yes. And I expect you to keep your trap shut and get your mind in the right place," Granddad said. His threat was clear.

Marcus cringed as he pictured his mother cowering in front of her father. Bile rose in his throat.

"Melvin has created a superwolf, Lora. Unstoppable." His father's words were filled with pride as though he were discussing some educational accomplishment rather than some strange subversive military coup planned by his grandfather. What were they called? The Romulus? Marcus's spine stiffened as he pondered what a superwolf might be.

"What's a superwolf? Why?" his mother asked, voicing Marcus's exact thoughts.

Melvin spoke again. "They're larger and stronger than the average shifter. Lora, I'm tired of taking orders from others. I'm sick of living in hiding. We've lived below the radar as a species for centuries. I have the financial backing now to make this possible. There are humans in high places who know about us. They're helping me. In return, I'll assist them."

Whatever the fuck his grandfather had planned, the details made Marcus go pale. His body shook with rage. He needed to get out of there, and fast. The last thing he wanted to do was to get caught and hauled into this mess.

How he'd lived twenty-six years oblivious to all this shit was beyond him, but he didn't have to live another minute on the wrong side of justice knowing what he now knew.

"Where's Marcus now?" his grandfather asked.

"Probably on his way over. I invited him for dinner," his mother said.

Thank God he'd gotten off work earlier than expected and come straight to his parents' home. He hated to think what might have happened if he'd been ten minutes too late for this powwow.

"Then I'll wait. We'll either convince him to come in, or take him against his will if need be."

Marcus eased away from his spot against the outside wall. He prayed not a single board in the porch squeaked to give him away as he inched toward the side railing. He didn't dare go back down the front steps. With one hand on the banister, he leaped over the top and landed firmly on the ground. Seconds later he was running into the woods behind his parents' house.

He couldn't take the chance of going home. Besides, he wouldn't be able to take anything with him anyway. He wasn't going to take a casual drive in his car to escape. The only option he had was to shift and go completely under the radar. Rogue.

He managed to dash more than a mile into the trees before he paused to shed his clothes and shift. The last thing he wanted was for anyone to easily figure out he'd run by encountering his clothing. He found a dip in the ground, buried everything he had, and covered it with debris and leaves. Over the years he'd run in these woods so many times, there was no way anyone would be able to track him. His scent was everywhere.

Shifting was quick and easy, and then he was on the move.

He lamented the loss of the life he'd built for himself over the last few years. His job as a contractor would quickly be snatched up by someone else when he didn't show up for work. It couldn't be helped.

Marcus was a grown man. No drugs had been in his system for six years, with the exception of that one weekend. He'd worked hard to build his life the way he wanted it, giving everything he had physically and emotionally to overcome his weird childhood. And he wasn't about to lose the ground he'd gained. Not even for family. Not for anybody.

He ran. Hard. His destination easy.

Texas.

Like his mother, Marcus would never believe the Spencers had anything to do with the kidnapping or harboring of anyone. His best option now was to go see for himself.

Spencer Ranch, three weeks later...

Heather heard the rattle only a second before she felt the stinging bite of small teeth entering her ankle. She yelped and jumped, but it was too late. Instant pain ran up her leg and froze her in her spot. "Fuck." She didn't dare move as she watched the venomous diamondback slither away.

Tears filled her eyes. She lifted her gaze toward the main ranch house. She was too far away to make it to the house. In fact, her leg hurt worse than any pain she'd ever experienced, and she lowered herself to her knees as the pain increased. As a human, the clock was ticking.

Heather shook her head. She needed to think. She gritted her teeth and then screamed. No one heard her. Why had she wandered so far from the corral and barn alone? She sat hard on her ass and grabbed her leg with both hands as though squeezing her calf would alleviate the searing pain.

Her eyes watered, blurring her vision. But she could see enough to watch her ankle swell rapidly around the two puncture wounds. "Dammit," she muttered.

Heather was a nurse. She needed to take a deep breath and calm herself. *Think.* Her life depended on it.

Her chest seized with fear. She could literally die right here on the ground. And who knew how long it would take for the Spencers to find her?

Heather flattened to the dirt. It wasn't a conscious choice. She was growing woozy. She bit down against the searing pain, curled onto her side, and grabbed her ankle with both hands.

Her ponytail whipped across her face, obscuring her vision, but she couldn't care enough to brush the locks away. Tears escaped to run down her cheeks, and she bit the inside of her lip to keep from screaming as she struggled against the burn in her leg and blinked back the dirt in her eyes. All she could see through the curtain of thick hair was the tall brush in which she lay hidden.

She tried to steady her breathing. Suddenly she had a moment of clarity. *Shift. You must shift. It's the only way.*

Dragging the last bit of energy she could manage, Heather called forth the shift. It took longer than usual, but she managed. Several seconds later she lay panting on the ground in wolf form, her clothes in tattered shreds around her. Her leg still hurt like a mother, but at least she wouldn't likely die.

As a wolf, she would heal faster. Her body was less likely to shut down from the venom.

She didn't move, afraid her legs wouldn't hold her up if she tried to stand. She closed her eyes against the glaring sun and let herself slip into sleep. If she died, perhaps she wouldn't even be aware of it. If she lived, at least in slumber she would give her body a fighting chance to heal.

～

Marcus paced inside the tree line. He'd wandered around the outskirts of the Spencer Ranch for three days now. He knew the best thing to do was to man up and head for the main house, but he hadn't conjured the courage yet.

A loud scream rent the air and made him jerk his head in the direction of the noise. A woman stood only a few dozen yards from him, long glorious red hair blowing behind her. How had he not noticed her? It wasn't like him to wander so close to the main section of the ranch.

Just as he was about to duck back between the trees and slink off deeper into the woods, he saw a look of sheer horror on her face. She cussed as he watched. Her red curls were held back by a ponytail, but hair blew across her features as she bent at the waist. And then she disappeared entirely from his view, collapsing onto her knees and then disappearing into the brush.

What the fuck?

Obviously she was in horrible pain, but from what? Could she have stepped on a trap?

Marcus turned to run deeper into the woods, but something told him to stay close. He sat on his haunches and sniffed the air, tipping his head back.

The woman was a shifter. He could discern that without much effort. And the fact wasn't shocking. He'd noticed only shifters on the ranch since he'd been watching them from afar.

He stared at the spot where the woman disappeared, silently cussing inside his head. He couldn't leave her there. *What the hell is she doing?*

Nothing. Silence. He watched for several minutes, beginning to think he'd completely hallucinated the redhead in the first place. Had she fallen into the Bermuda Triangle?

Marcus inched forward as though pulled to do so by an invisible string. As he got closer, he heard a low moaning sound. She was definitely injured. And he smelled wolf. She'd shifted. Good. At least she'd had enough sense to take her lupine form. Whatever injury she'd sustained would heal faster in wolf form.

Yards away still, Marcus crept forward. He smelled her distinctly, long before he saw her. And he stopped moving.

His chest pounded. His ears twitched. He lifted his nose into the air to get a better scent.

Holy mother of God. She's my mate.

Marcus sat on his haunches. He had no other choice. If he hadn't, he would have collapsed onto them anyway. He jerked his head in every direction, suddenly aware someone could spot him. No one was around. He almost wished they were. His mate needed help.

Pulled into action, Marcus lowered his body out of sight and crawled forward until he reached his mate's body. The first thing he saw was her gorgeous red fur, the same shade of her human hair. The second thing he saw was her badly swollen leg.

Had she been bitten by something? He nudged her paw with his nose, seeing the blood caked in her fur. He licked at the wound. Snake. Had to be. Shit. For this kind of damage in such a short span of time, it had to have been a rattlesnake. He could taste the venom on his tongue and spat it out on the ground.

Marcus circled to her face and felt her steady breathing as it wafted onto his snout. She was alive. He lay alongside her, keeping his nose right next to hers. If there was any change, he would know. As long as she slept off the venom, she would be safe. All he needed to do was keep an eye on her ankle and ensure the swelling didn't progress up her leg, and she would be fine. Her wolf would fight the infection. It was rare for a shifter to succumb to such an injury, especially if they managed to change into wolf form as quickly as she had.

It would hurt for several days, but she'd pull through.

She had to.

For over an hour Marcus lay next to his mate, learning her scent and every tiny move she made in her restless slumber. She moaned every few minutes, a sound he hoped to never hear again in this lifetime. It wasn't the good kind of moan he hoped to rend from her in bed, but rather a pained expression of discomfort.

And what the hell was he thinking? He couldn't take a mate right now. He hadn't been with anyone in over a year. He wasn't ready.

He glanced at the red wolf's leg every few minutes. No change. The danger had passed.

He lifted his head toward the main house. No one came to look for her. He wasn't sure if he was relieved or not. On the one hand he wanted to be the one by her side. On the other hand, she needed medical care to alleviate her pain.

Marcus peered toward the barn. He could shift and go get help for her. Hell, he could go in wolf form. But would anyone follow him? They didn't know him. That was his fault for hanging back so many days. He could have gone to the front door three days ago, and then he wouldn't be in this predicament.

He shook his head and settled it back down next to the gorgeous red wolf. He inhaled deeply. He'd never expected to find a true mate in this lifetime, not after the experience he'd had at The Gathering. Fifteen months had gone by since that horrific weekend. Intellectually he knew everything that had come out of his mouth over the weekend had been the result of the drugs, but it didn't keep him from cringing every time he thought about his actions.

Since arriving at the Spencer Ranch, he'd done nothing but pace along the fringes of the property, courage evading him. Fate had a very strange sense of humor.

And now he was faced with a mate? What were the odds? He momentarily doubted his instincts. Was she really his?

She has to be. This feeling doesn't come close to resembling the sensation you had with those women at The Gathering. That had been lust brought on by some sort of hormone injection. You aren't drugged now, big guy. You're clearheaded, and this woman is yours.

He growled in frustration, quickly stopping himself from disturbing his mate.

She was injured. The last thing she needed was to wake up and find some rogue wolf peering over her and demanding to claim her for his own.

And what was he thinking? No way could he mate with this woman. She knew nothing about him—his skeletons. Fate was beyond humor. She was a cruel ball of laughter today.

The scent of this sweet shifter next to him seemed to seep into his bloodstream as though they were already mated. He would know her anywhere. It wasn't a random infatuation masked as lust. He really felt connected to her.

Still. Don't act rashly. Enough people have been hurt.

The wolf squirmed. She opened her eyes, blinking away the dust. The moment she saw Marcus next to her, she flinched. She breathed heavier for several moments. Marcus let her adjust to the shock.

She panted, her eyes wide. Did she recognize the call?

He held his breath.

When she lifted a paw and settled it over his, he nearly groaned.

And then she winced, drawing back her paw and struggling to wiggle free of his proximity.

Marcus scooted back, giving her space.

She twisted her head down to her injured paw and licked the wound. Seemingly satisfied she was healing properly, she dropped her head back down to a resting position, her snout over her paw.

She stared at Marcus again, cocking her head one way in assessment.

Marcus returned her gaze, not breaking eye contact. Too bad neither of them could communicate with the other. Or perhaps this way was better. Gave her a chance to acclimate to her new reality before he claimed her.

Now that she was conscious, he needed to get her to safety. Marcus inched closer to her again. He nudged her front paws. Hopefully she would take the hint.

The gorgeous red wolf was much smaller than him. She glanced down at her paws and then tried to lift herself. She wobbled, but she would be able to limp toward the barn at least. It was the closest building.

Marcus nudged her again. He couldn't risk shifting, even though he wanted nothing more than to take his human form, lift her in his arms, and carry her to her people.

But the risk was too high. He didn't know these people well enough. He had no way of knowing if they would accept him. And he couldn't take that kind of chance, especially since he'd learned one of them was his mate. He needed more information before he revealed himself.

Instead, Marcus nudged her again, this time pushing her face toward the barn. If he could get her to the entrance, someone would find her quickly.

Limping forward on three legs, the red wolf teetered. Marcus could do little to help, but he stayed by her weak side, allowing her to rest against his larger body when she needed a break. It took several minutes. She glanced at him many times. Her eyes were glazed. Probably from the pain.

When they finally reached the entrance to the barn, Marcus heard voices inside. He didn't have much time. He licked his mate's front paw, lowered his head in sorrow, and then turned to run, hell-bent on making it to the tree line before anyone saw him.

It was the hardest thing he'd ever done.

He left her. His chest burned. He wasn't sure he even breathed for several minutes as he jumped back into the trees and kept running. He'd meant to turn and watch, to make sure she was found. But he couldn't bring himself to stop. He needed to burn off the rage inside him.

What was he so bent out of shape about all of a sudden? She was his mate. He should be by her side. It superseded his doubts about how the Spencers would receive him.

But he needed to gather his thoughts and make a rational decision. Nothing hasty would cut it. It wasn't going to be easy coming clean. After all, one of the women living on the ranch was Mackenzie Davis, the first woman he'd accosted at that damn Gathering, insisting she was his mate. Besides the uphill battle he would face convincing the Spencers he was on their side, he'd come here seeking refuge, and he would have the added challenge of facing his past actions. He'd always wondered when that weekend would bite him in the ass. Apparently now.

Why should these people believe anything he said? He was the grandson of the enemy. And on top of everything, he'd just met his true mate.

He wasn't 100% sure about the Spencers and their involvement in whatever was happening to his species. His gut told him they were good people. He'd met them on many occasions over the years. Was it possible they were as deeply involved in something as clandestine as his own family? That remained to be seen. After watching them for several days, he didn't have all the answers.

Everything that had happened to him in his life led to this moment in time. Only fear crept in. Fear of rejection. Fear of being found guilty of past injustices. Fear of betrayal…

Because it all boiled down to that. Marcus Cunningham had been betrayed. Betrayed by his grandfather, his father, and indirectly his mother. And he wasn't about to let it happen again.

CHAPTER 2

Heather awoke with a start. She bolted to a sitting position, gasping for air, only seconds before becoming aware of the sharp pain in her left ankle.

"You're awake." The sweet voice from the other side of the room made her lift her gaze from the propped swollen leg with the two sharp teeth marks to find Kenzie rushing toward her. "Don't move so much." She set a hand on Heather's back and helped her lie back down. "It'll hurt worse." Kenzie was the sweetest woman Heather had ever met. Mated to the oldest Spencer son, Drake, she'd come to the ranch last summer after The Gathering.

Heather winced. "Like a motherfucker," she muttered.

Kenzie smiled and brought a drink of water to Heather's lips. "Here. Try to drink. It'll flush out the toxins."

"It was a diamondback."

"Yep. That's pretty obvious."

Heather tried to remember the details. "I was walking across from the pasture."

Kenzie furrowed her brow. "How did you get to the barn, then?"

"The barn? I... I don't know." And then she remembered. The details crashed around her. She bolted to sitting again. "Where is he?"

"Who?"

"The wolf who helped me." She shuffled the sheets off her good leg, intent on pulling herself to standing.

Kenzie held out both hands to steady Heather and keep her from getting up. "Nobody mentioned another wolf when they carried you in. You were in wolf form yourself, though. You must have shifted when you were bitten. Good thing too. Probably saved your life."

"But the dark wolf..." Heather leaned back down, all the air leaving her lungs. Had she imagined him? Was it possible she'd hallucinated a mate into existence from the poison?

"I'm sorry, honey." Kenzie stuffed the sheet back under Heather's good leg, making sure not to jostle the injured one and keep it lifted. "I'll ask Drake if he saw anyone, but you were pretty out of it when they brought you in the house. Maybe you imagined him?"

Heather closed her eyes. She couldn't believe she'd dreamed him.

"Here. Take some Tylenol. It will lessen the pain."

Heather opened her eyes again, only a slit, enough to let Kenzie slip three pills into her mouth and then swallow a long drink of water. It tasted like heaven. So sweet... She was so thirsty...

"Good. Drink as much as you can."

Heather downed the glass and then let her head flop back onto the pillow.

"Rest. Your mind will be clearer when you wake up next."

Heather let sleep pull her under again, but she was agitated this time. All she could see was dark fur and deep brown eyes peering so close to her she could see into the other wolf's soul. His gaze was sad, desperate, longing. He was hers. She knew it. Even if she did imagine him into existence.

The next time Heather woke up, the sun was lower in the sky. It was evening, and she was alone. She glanced around the room. Nothing was different. A large pitcher of water and a glass sat next to her on the bedside table. She tried to lick her lips, but found her mouth too dry to attempt it.

She swiveled her upper body and managed to pour herself a glass of water without spilling too much. She gulped it down as though she'd been lost in the desert for weeks. According to her mouth, she had.

The door opened, and Heather switched her gaze to the entrance. Natalie Spencer came in with a cheery smile. "You're up."

"Not really. I feel horrible. Even my head hurts."

"Yeah. But you're so lucky." She sat on the edge of the bed. "Most of the swelling went down before you shifted to human form. Scared the poop out of the boys when they found you outside the barn, out cold and gasping for air." The woman's concerned brow calmed Heather. Natalie had been a mother figure to

Heather ever since she'd arrived on the ranch weeks ago.

Heather tried to remember the details, not wanting to look like a complete fool again. All she could see in her mind was the dark wolf. Her mate. He'd helped her to the spot as best he could. Where had he gone?

"Don't stress about the details." Natalie patted her good leg. "All that matters is you managed to crawl to the barn. And we found you."

Ah, so Kenzie had spoken to Natalie. She was pandering to her now.

Heather shook her head. "It wasn't in my imagination. A black wolf helped me. You need to find him."

Natalie paused. "You really think so? Nobody saw any wolves besides you."

"Well, nobody saw me either, but I was there. I was way out by the tree line. Walking. Enjoying the weather. When I was bit, I twisted all around. I even screamed. Nobody saw me." Heather sat forward, her voice growing stronger. "So isn't it possible there's another wolf out there nobody saw?" She grabbed Natalie's hand. "I'm not imagining this, Mrs. Spencer. I'm telling you he was there. He came out of the tree line, helped me back to the barn, and then..." She inhaled deeply. "Why did he leave?"

"That's the million dollar question."

"Please send someone to look for him. Maybe he's injured also. Maybe he's in the trees alone." She couldn't think of a single reason why her savior had left her. Who did that?

If it sounded odd to Natalie, it sounded dumber to Heather in her own mind. She hadn't mentioned what she presumed the lone wolf to be to her.

He's my mate. She was certain. "Please." She squeezed Natalie's hand. "It would mean a lot to me. Just send someone to look."

Natalie smiled and nodded. "I will. And I'll bring you some soup. Hang tight." Natalie stood. She hesitated when she reached the door, but she didn't turn back.

Would she keep her word? Heather wasn't sure, but she'd never known the woman to lie. It wasn't in her nature. Heather had been on the ranch for weeks now, ever since she'd been rescued from some strange organization called the Romulus. The last few months were insanity. After being kidnapped by two men she'd never met and whisked away to some remote area of Oregon, she'd been drugged and kept locked in a basement.

She'd never expected anyone to find her, but she'd been one of the lucky ones. Her parents had called The Head Council almost immediately, and she'd been added to the planned sting operation and picked up less than a week after her kidnapping, simultaneously with eleven other women around the country. Some had been held much longer than her. Some had been much less fortunate.

Heather was on the road to recovery. All twelve women had come to the Spencer Ranch to meet with counselors and recuperate together in a group setting. It was discovered half of them had a GPS chip inserted in their necks. Heather cringed even now as she considered the day they'd all held their breath while a medical team examined them and removed those damn devices.

Heather hadn't been among them. Did it mean she was less valuable to the Romulus? No one was sure. The six with GPS locators had been moved to other locations. Heather remained on the ranch with the rest, but all of them had soon trickled back to their homes.

Heather wasn't in a hurry. She'd just graduated from college with her nursing degree when she was kidnapped. Never fond of the small town in Oregon where she grew up, she'd been filling out applications to hospitals all over the country. She was free to go anywhere she wanted.

When Natalie offered for her to stay in the main house until she got her feet under her, she'd easily taken the opportunity. She loved the ranch. The Spencers were the nicest people. As an only child, she'd never been around so many loving people. The volume and laughter melted her heart.

Not that her parents hadn't been the best parents she could ask for. But they had no other children. They hadn't exposed her to large cities or crowds. Her friends had all moved on, and she wanted to do the same.

Heather shook herself from her reverie when Natalie bustled back into the room with a tray. "Soup's on."

Heather's mouth watered. It smelled fantastic. She pulled herself to a sitting position. She was starving, and her stomach growled in agreement as soon as Natalie set the tray on her lap.

"It's canned chicken noodle soup, but I thought that would be easiest on your stomach right now. Tomorrow you can try something more substantial." Natalie pulled up a chair. "Go ahead. Eat while it's hot."

Heather took the first sip and moaned. "Perfect. Thank you so much. For everything." She lifted her gaze. "I don't know where I'd be without you and your family." Tears clouded her eyes, but she held them at bay.

Natalie waved away her praise. "Not a problem. You're like my own daughter now. Nothing I wouldn't do for anyone." She paused. "Scott and Jerrod shifted and went to look for your black wolf."

Heather blinked. "Thank you," she whispered. "It means a lot to me. I swear I'm not crazy." Having Natalie's youngest sons looking for her mate was better than nothing.

"Never thought you were." Natalie smiled.

If they were all just humoring her, she didn't care. As long as they found the black wolf, that was all that mattered. A chill raced down her spine. *He's mine.* Her certainty grew with each passing moment. She wanted him found, and she wanted answers.

Heather slept restlessly that night, in part due to the throbbing in her leg, and in part due to the mysterious disappearance of her mate. The Spencers had not had any success finding anyone near the main ranch property.

But now, with dawn creeping in, she was wide awake. As she stared at the horizon through the window of her room in the main house, she heard a commotion. It started far away and grew louder as whoever it was approached her room.

She was lifting her upper body to sit when the door flew open and Natalie's mate, Jerome, burst into the room with his son Scott on his heels. Her gaze immediately shifted to the black wolf pushing past them both, however. He bounded into the room and skidded to a stop when he spotted her. He cocked his head to one side and sat on his haunches for a moment. If wolves could smile, he was doing so.

"I'm sorry, Heather," Scott began. "He was roaming around outside when I went to the barn. He made it clear he wanted in the house even shifted." Scott's voice was fearful.

"It's okay." Heather didn't take her eyes off the black wolf.

Suddenly he bounded onto the bed in one leap and sat at her feet.

"Oh," she gasped, leaning back.

He was ragged around the edges, in need of a bath. He was also invading her space. But he was hers.

"Oh," Jerome repeated. Even in wolf form, there would be no way to hide the fact he was her mate from anyone. They would all sense it. "Now I see the urgency." He chuckled as he stepped forward. He took the wolf's jaw in his hand and turned his face, forcing the black wolf to meet his gaze. "You get one warning, fellow. I don't know you, and I have no idea why you haven't shifted, but if you hurt one hair on this woman's head, your ass is mine. You hear?"

The black wolf nodded. He transferred his gaze back to Heather and stared at her.

"Give us a minute," Heather said. She watched as the black wolf made himself at home at her feet.

Scott spoke up next. "Are you sure? We don't know anything about him. He could harm you."

"If he wanted to hurt me, he would have done so yesterday. He saved my life and brought me to you." Heather didn't look at Jerome or Scott as she explained. She didn't feel the stress they felt. She was perfectly calm gazing at her mate. She knew instinctively he would protect her against any enemy on the Earth. She wasn't in any harm in his care.

Except maybe for her heart. His narrowed gaze gave her a chill, and he never stopped watching her.

Jerome and Scott left the room, shutting the door behind them. They mumbled something about being closeby, but Heather barely listened.

She stared at her mate, clearer than she'd been in almost twenty-four hours.

He stared back.

"Well, are you going to just lie there?" She narrowed her gaze, waiting for him to shift. "I wouldn't mind seeing you in human form. Perhaps we could even have a conversation," she sassed.

The black wolf lifted his head and ducked his nose to look down at her, as if to say, "I'll damn well shift when I'm good and ready."

"Seriously?"

He continued to stare. His breath landed on her ankle, tickling her skin.

She pulled it away from his face, only to be brought up short, wincing at the pain.

He mewled and scooted back, blinking at her with sorrowful eyes.

Ah, not so tough after all. She stored the information away for safekeeping. He might be playing the big bad wolf, but he also cringed to see her suffer.

"Fine. I'll go first. I'm Heather. Heather Peters. I'm from Oregon." She paused.

His ears had perked up.

"Wait. Why am I telling you all about myself when you've shown no interest in reciprocating?" She threw her hands down and then drew the covers up higher on her body, realizing she lay there in nothing more than a tank top with no bra.

In fact, the wolf lowered his gaze to her chest as she wiggled to get farther under the covers.

"Are you kidding? You don't get to ogle me, big guy." She rolled her eyes and leaned back. "Geez. How did I get so lucky?"

Marcus watched her every expression. Heather Peters was gorgeous. He couldn't stop panting at her feet. Her red hair was disheveled around her face, the curls falling in every direction even though she tried repeatedly to tuck them behind her ears. Freckles dotted her nose and cheeks, enticing him when she scrunched up her face. Her eyes bored into him, the green depths seeming to reveal her deepest, darkest secrets.

When she flattened and stared at the ceiling, he settled more comfortably at her feet. He hadn't eaten since early yesterday, but he could go a long time in wolf form without food.

What he couldn't do was stay away from Heather. He'd tried. All night he'd wandered the woods, pacing. But by morning he knew it was a lost battle. He needed to be near her. Even if he didn't shift, he needed to know she was okay. Healing. Recuperating. The rest he would figure out as he went along. First, he could at least get a better feeling for these people inside their home rather than pacing the edge of the forest.

Not to mention the fact she was bound to tell them about him. He decided he was better off coming forward rather than being found roaming the property.

He had enough hurdles to surmount without adding creepy stalker to the mix.

What he hadn't figured into the equation was the way her presence would slam him in the chest and take his breath away. In human form in a trapped room, it was worse. She was his. Did she know that? She seemed interested in getting to know him, but she hadn't specifically said anything about them being mates.

"Thank you," she muttered as she pulled her damn sheet higher.

For what? For rescuing her? He hadn't really done anything. She'd done all the work. All he'd done was lie next to her and then nudge her into action.

Someone knocked at the door, and Marcus lifted his

head and swung toward the opening, immediately going on the defense.

"You doing all right in here?" It was yet another brother. He'd ascertained there were at least three brothers. Though he thought he remembered there being a fourth from his youth. They all looked like their father, so it was easy to figure out.

The latest man glanced at Marcus and furrowed his brow. He came farther into the room. "Is he going to shift?"

"Hmm. I'm not sure. He's not saying." Heather grinned, and Marcus nearly swallowed his tongue when a gorgeous smile spread across her face, lighting up her eyes until they sparkled.

The newcomer smirked. "Guess not. Weird." He turned toward Marcus. "I'm Drake. I guess you met my dad and my brother, Scott." He stuck his hands in his pockets and rocked on his heels as he turned back to face Heather. "He's a chatty one, huh."

"Yeah. I can't rest with all his yammering." She smiled again.

Marcus would gladly stay in wolf form forever if it meant seeing the twinkle in her eye.

Drake reached a hand forward, and Marcus growled before he could stop himself, lifting up on all fours.

Drake lifted both arms up. "Easy, fellow. I was just going to pour her some water. Her lips are dry. She hasn't had enough to drink since she was bitten." He slowly lowered his hands until he picked up the pitcher and poured a glass, only taking his gaze off Marcus for short instances.

Heather sat up, pulling her legs away from Marcus's snout. She narrowed her gaze at him. She wasn't laughing now. "Stop it."

He conceded marginally, knowing his actions were unreasonable. Everything about this decision to come forward was unreasonable. He'd done so for purely selfish reasons in the end. He needed to know if it was true. That this woman, Heather Peters, was indeed his mate. It didn't matter he wasn't about to shift for her. He simply wanted to be certain she was safe, healing…and his.

Now that you know, what are you going to do with that information, big guy?

"Kinda protective, isn't he?"

"Yeah." She looked directly at Marcus while she spoke.

Drake handed Heather a glass of water. He turned toward Marcus. "Hey, if you want to get the next glass, be my guest." And he turned and strolled from the room.

Marcus panted. He *did* want to get the next glass. He wouldn't, but he wanted to. There were a lot of things he wanted, but life didn't always throw the best curve balls. Claiming a mate at this juncture was beyond selfish. Marcus had nothing to offer this woman except a pile of horrific information concerning his own flesh and blood. She would freak out if she knew half of the shit he'd been a party to.

"So, how long are we going to hang out like this?" She set her glass down and crossed her arms. The blankets were tucked tightly against her chest. He wished she'd let them fall.

He sat back down with a sigh, jerking his attention back to his mate. He couldn't have answered her if he wanted to. Right now he wanted to stare at her and make sure she was safe. He hadn't thought past that yet.

She's safe. You can see that. Why are you still here?

Heather scooted back down and held his gaze for a long time. Finally her eyes fluttered shut, and she slept again.

Marcus inched forward slowly. He wanted to be as close to her as possible. There was plenty of space alongside her, and she couldn't protest while asleep... He also couldn't bring himself to leave her yet...

Someone was petting him... It felt so good, like his mother used to do when he was a small child. Slowly he opened his eyes, suddenly aware he'd fallen asleep. It had been a dream.

Only it wasn't a dream. It was Heather. He stared into her face. Her eyes were closed, her mouth parted in a sweet position, indicating she was deep asleep. But her hand was on top of him, hugging him to her.

And he'd never been as happy as that moment. In sleep she craved his proximity. She'd pulled him closer, or perhaps she'd scooted toward him.

The room was bright. Midday. Marcus needed water. He eyed the pitcher on the bedside table with envy.

Heather stirred. A soft moan escaped her lips, and then she dug her hand deeper into his fur. A moment passed before she became alert enough to realize her position.

She bolted upright, releasing him. Her chest heaved. She brushed her hair from her face. "You scared the crap out of me."

Marcus watched her breasts as they rose and fell, her nipples erect under the tight tank top. She was sexy as hell, and he couldn't do a damn thing about it in this state. *Or in any state, asshole.*

"Still in wolf form, I see." She inched away from him. "Aren't you hungry? Thirsty?"

He was. But he didn't move, not wanting her scent to disappear.

Heather shoved at him. "Get off the bed, you mutt. I need to use the bathroom."

Marcus hesitated. If he could have laughed at her term for him, he would have. He glanced at her ankle. It looked much better. She could probably walk. He bounded from the bed, landing on all fours. He sat on his haunches as she swung her legs around and threw her blankets back.

Heather winced as she set her feet on the floor. "My bladder's going to burst," she muttered. She tentatively put pressure on her foot and then stood. "Ow. Son of a bitch, that hurts."

Marcus leaped forward, though he hadn't a clue what he could do to help.

As soon as she steadied herself enough to avoid falling, Marcus lifted his gaze from her feet. And God almighty. He sucked in a breath. Even in wolf form, he reacted to her.

Heather wore nothing but silk panties and a tank top. It was askew, almost revealing one breast. She hobbled forward, holding on to the bedside table as she moved toward the attached bathroom.

Marcus couldn't move. He was in her way, but he was frozen in his spot, mesmerized by her sexy body. Her pale legs and arms matched her face, all wide expanse of glorious smooth skin dotted with freckles.

When she couldn't get past him, she turned toward him. "Move. Geez." And then she glanced down at herself. She righted her shirt and rolled her eyes. "Oh for fuck's sake. Have you never seen a woman in her underwear? Lord, wolfboy." She set her hands on her hips, no longer doing her best to cover herself. "Dude. I don't know if you realize this, but it seems you're my mate. I can't for the love of God figure out why you're sitting at my feet all doggy like, but move so I can use the bathroom."

Marcus hopped up and did as she said, inwardly chuckling at her endearments. Wolfboy? Mutt? Doggy? If he'd been in human form, he would have bust a gut laughing. She was right. This was absurd. But he didn't have the courage to change. And until this moment, he hadn't had any intention of changing ever. Could he do it? Leave this woman and walk away?

Heather passed him and hobbled to the bathroom. She shut the door, leaving him alone in the room. He glanced around her space. It was sparsely furnished, and there was nothing to indicate it was lived in full time by any particular person. The comforter at the foot of the bed was floral. Was Heather a floral kind of girl? He didn't think so.

This wasn't her room. It was a guest room. Did she not live in the main house? She didn't appear to be related to the people who'd come in and out of the room. A bit too formal. Maybe she'd been visiting.

Or maybe she's one of the women kidnapped by the North American Reserves last month. Marcus held his breath as he considered the option. It was possible, though he hadn't seen evidence of any of the others. He hadn't seen more than three women on the property at any time.

He had to agree with his mother. No way were the Spencers involved in something sinister. He'd been here for hours and no one had yet been anything other than polite and accepting, even though he'd given them no reason whatsoever to trust him.

Heather hobbled back into the room. She opened a drawer and pulled out a few things. She ignored him completely, and then she headed back for the restroom. Seconds later, he heard water running. The shower.

If she hadn't closed the door entirely, he didn't believe he would have been able to keep from nosing it open and watching her strip out of her meager clothing and duck under the spray. He licked his chops thinking about it.

In wolf form his ardor was at bay, but barely. If he shifted now, he wouldn't be able to control himself. He'd never wanted a woman as badly as Heather Peters in his life. And her feisty mannerisms and cocky mouth made him itch to claim her immediately. He couldn't believe how strong the call to mate could be. Overpowering to the point of insanity.

He panted, staring at the bathroom door. He needed to shift, on a visceral level. He needed to claim this woman almost as bad as he needed his next breath. No, worse. Instead he growled low in his throat as he listened to the water running down the drain, knowing his mate was naked behind the door. Damn Fate and Her wicked, witty self.

CHAPTER 3

Heather returned from the bathroom and rolled her eyes at the wolf still lying on the floor. She decided not to speak to him for a while. See how he liked it. Ignoring him, she left the room, limping toward the kitchen. She felt him on her heels, but she didn't turn around.

"Heather." Natalie bustled over to help her, grabbing her arm with one hand and leading her to the kitchen table. "You look much better. Not as pale."

Heather took a chair and propped her leg up on another. "I feel more alive. I took a shower." It went without saying since her hair was damp and hanging in long ringlets, completely natural.

The wolf sat at her feet.

"You must be starving."

"Yes, ma'am. And it smells so good in here."

"Vegetable soup. I thought it would hit the spot. I know it's technically too hot outside for soup these days, but when I'm feeling under the weather, I like it anyway."

"Yes." She licked her lips. "You're correct."

Natalie returned with a bowl, a chunk of fresh-baked bread, and a glass of iced tea. She took a seat next to Heather.

"So…"

Heather shook her head and nodded toward her feet. Hopefully Natalie would get her drift. Maybe if she stopped pandering to the stupid wolf, he would come around.

Or maybe it wasn't that he didn't want to shift. Maybe he couldn't.

Shit. "Could a wolf spend so much time shifted that they can't shift back, do you suppose?"

Natalie's eyelids rose. "I suppose. We were just discussing that possibility in fact. I've never known anyone who did, though." She glanced under the table. "Frankly, I don't think it's been too long. He's a little ragged, but not the way I'd expect him to look if he'd been in this form for years."

"True." Heather blew on a bite and sipped it. Heaven. She moaned. The wolf lifted his face. "So he's just an ass."

Now he growled.

Natalie smiled. "I wouldn't go that far. He's awfully protective. Not leaving your side. He knows."

"Yeah, he knows all right. Thought he might have a coronary when I got out of bed in my undies."

Natalie laughed. "Hmm. If that didn't do it…"

"Maybe he didn't like what he saw."

The wolf growled again.

"Okay so not that."

The men suddenly burst into the room from outside, letting the screen door slam behind them. The wolf sat up on his haunches and eased closer to her leg.

"You're awake," Jerome said.

"Yep."

He glanced at the floor. "And your mate hasn't shifted yet."

"Nope."

The men all took seats at the table, and Natalie went to the stove to bring over the pot of soup.

"Do you know how hot it is out there, Mom?" Scott asked.

"Shut your mouth. This is for Heather. If you don't want it, make a sandwich."

Scott lifted his arms. "Sorry. That was rude."

"Very." Natalie resumed her spot at the table. She must have already eaten. She hadn't set a place for herself.

Scott, Jerome, and Jerrod, the youngest Spencer at only twelve, started eating.

"Did Drake go back to his own place for lunch?" Natalie asked them.

"Yeah." Jerome swallowed his bite. "Said he needed to help Kenzie with the baby. She apparently didn't get much sleep last night."

"That poor girl. I'll go relieve her in a while so she can take a nap."

"Maybe I'll go with you," Heather said.

The wolf perked up at the pronouncement. She'd

known he would. In a moment he settled back at her feet. She'd only said it to get a rise out of him. It worked.

It didn't last long, however. Jerome spoke again. "I've been thinking. Do you think it's possible your wolf has been drugged? That could explain why he hasn't shifted. He could be held in a suspended state and can't reach beyond the drugs yet."

Heather almost fell out of her chair when her wolf jumped to both feet and stared at Jerome. Bingo.

Jerome smiled. "Okay then. That's a possibility. Perhaps he escaped the Romulus and hasn't been able to shift yet."

"Why do you suppose he came here?" Heather wondered if he knew about the ranch and came for a similar reason. Refuge. But that didn't explain his reluctance to shift.

Heather set her hand on the wolf's head and wove her fingers into his fur. She hated the idea, but considering how many shifters had fallen under the influence of the Romulus, it wasn't far-fetched to assume this wolf had been among the victims.

"If he's been receiving the same drugs as the other members of the Romulus, why isn't he extraordinarily large and strong?"

The wolf stiffened.

"Sorry. Didn't mean it as an insult." She held his head and tipped his jaw up to meet his gaze. "Have you seen those superwolves?"

He blinked at her. *Okay, maybe not.*

Jerome interjected again. "Anything's possible. Now that we know there's some genetics involved, it's possible he didn't have the right genomes to convert. A simple blood test should tell us if he's been receiving anything unusual." Jerome looked at the wolf. "Would you agree to that?"

The wolf stood rigid. He didn't move for several moments. Finally he nodded subtly.

Heather felt relieved. *Making progress here.* "Do you think you'll find the same drugs in him I had in me?"

The wolf flinched, baring his teeth.

Heather took his head in her hands. "Relax, big guy. I'm safe now. And you are too. The Spencers are good people. Whatever happened to you in the past, you can trust everyone on this ranch."

Jerome shook his head. "I doubt we'll find the same drugs in your wolf. I think the goal of the Romulus must have something to do with making the males stronger and the females weaker."

The wolf growled.

Jerome chuckled. "He knows things. It's not a coincidence he's here."

Heather gripped his fur tighter. "Maybe he heard about this ranch being used as a refuge for women."

She couldn't deduce anything from his reaction to her statement. She'd have to wait for him to shift to get more answers.

When they finished lunch, Jerome went to the barn for several minutes to retrieve supplies. With all the horses they had, they kept a full supply of basic medical equipment. He returned with a syringe and a few vials. He handed them to Heather. "You should do it. You're the nurse around here, and he's likely to bite my arm off if I try."

Heather turned her chair a few inches and lowered her stiff leg to the ground to square up with the black wolf. He didn't move. He stared at her with wide eyes. "Can I have your paw?" She held out a hand, and he lifted his front leg to her thigh. "Just a blood draw. These guys can send it to a lab and get some answers." Her fingers shook. Drawing blood from a random stranger or a farm animal was one thing. Inflicting pain, no matter how minor, on her mate was another. Especially without his verbal commitment.

But he didn't flinch.

Natalie handed her a cotton swab, which Heather used to clean a spot on his front leg. Steadying her arm, she slowly pierced her wolf's skin and drew out three vials of blood.

She looked him in the eye when she was done. "Okay?"

He stared at her, narrowing his gaze as if to say, "How weak do I look?"

"I think he needs a drink." At the very least. She'd hoped to lure him into shifting with thirst, but if it was beyond his control, that would be cruel.

Natalie grabbed a dish, filled it with water, and set it by the back door. "Try not to get water all over the floor, big guy. I'm the one who has to mop it."

The wolf padded across the floor. Heather's heart ached. What if he couldn't shift? What would it mean for her life? "I need some air." Heather lifted herself up and limped toward the door next to her mate.

"Are you sure you're okay?" Natalie asked.

"I'm fine. Getting better by the second. In fact I think I'll find a nice, quiet, snake-free area and shift again. That should help finish off the healing." What she really wanted to do was get her mate out of the house. In wolf form he couldn't possibly be comfortable for such a long time inside.

Heather walked outside into the afternoon heat and immediately thought better of her plan. But her mate had perked up at the idea and lobbed ahead of her, glancing back every few seconds to make sure she was following. "I'm coming, big guy." She followed him to the tree line and then sat on a stump to remove her clothes. "Turn around. I know I joked about my underwear earlier, but I'm not getting naked in front of a man who hasn't managed to reciprocate, wolf form or not."

The wolf sat and faced toward the barn as though he were on guard. In a way he was.

Heather made a pile of her clothes and quickly shifted. She nudged her mate, tucking her nose up under his front paw.

His eyes danced as he turned to her. And then he pounced, flattening her to the ground in submission, belly up. He held her down with one paw.

Fine. Got it. You're the alpha. You can assert your authority in that area as soon as you shift. Too bad she had no way to communicate her thoughts with him. The only thing she could do was stay still and let him assert himself. In a strange warped way, she was turned on by his dominance.

Shifters didn't mate in their wolf form. Their minds were advanced even shifted. It wasn't something she would ever do. But she was nevertheless attracted to what small portion of his personality she was privy to in his natural form.

He couldn't talk to her, but he demonstrated his strength and virility anyway.

∾

Marcus stared down at his gorgeous mate, his heart pounding, his chest heaving. He held her steady for longer than necessary, hoping to ensure she understood he wasn't some dumb mutt. He was her mate.

Not that he was an ass, but he wasn't the pushover she may have perceived him to be.

He'd conceded to the bloodwork for several reasons. To do otherwise would have been suspicious. If they happened to find traces of some substance from years ago or even last year, it would only indicate he too was a victim. If not, he would be cleared of any possible ulterior motives the Spencers may suspect of him concerning Heather. Hell, he would be relieved to have the confirmation he was not under the influence of any substance affecting his knowledge that Heather was his true mate.

Now, if he could get her healed and then keep her safe, he'd be one hundred times more relaxed. Shifting could wait. The snake bite had shaved years off his life. Adding the knowledge she'd been drugged made his blood boil.

He'd nearly pounced on her when he'd come inside the house, shoving the Spencers out of the way to make sure she was safe and healing. How on earth he'd thought he could leave her and walk away into the woods, he couldn't imagine. It hadn't taken him long to wander back toward the main house, worry eating at his gut.

The Spencers were right about one thing, it had been a while since he'd shifted. And Natalie was astute about his state also. It hadn't been so long that he was a bedraggled mess. He was matted for sure, but not beyond repair. Nothing a shower and a comb wouldn't fix.

Marcus released Heather and nudged her to stand. He pawed at her hind leg, hoping to ascertain the level of her discomfort.

Heather picked up the afflicted paw and wiggled it. She nodded as she set it down, and then she took off running into the tree line.

The little imp.

Marcus bounded after her. What if she got bit again? Or fell? Or couldn't make it back?

Since when do you worry so much about someone else's safety?

Since I met my mate.

She didn't go far before pausing to rest her hind leg. She plopped down in a meadow and lolled in the sun. Marcus glanced around, unsure about the level of their safety. Surely Heather knew what she was doing. He hoped she wasn't foolish enough to put herself in danger. She hadn't done anything yet to concern him to that level, but he barely knew her.

And he wasn't convinced about the safety level of the ranch yet. There were a few members of the North American Reserves milling around at all times, probably remnants of whatever had gone down on the ranch before he'd arrived. NAR could only do so much. They had a few guys staying in one of the cabins on the property, but however many others had been there before, they were gone now.

He feared whatever army his grandfather had assembled.

He attempted to piece together Heather's story. She was from Oregon, so it meant she'd traveled quite a distance to get to the ranch in northwest Texas. And this family was not her own.

She'd spoken of women using the ranch as a refuge. That part fit what he suspected. So, where were they now?

Since she'd mentioned being drugged herself, he figured she had to have been one of the women captured by this group his grandfather spearheaded called the Romulus and given experimental drugs. He couldn't come up with a reason why she was the last one staying on the ranch. Living in the main house in fact.

They had so much in common. Too bad he couldn't tell her everything he knew.

Had they received the same drugs? Under what pretense had she been told they were necessary?

His grandfather mentioned superwolves coming

here for a battle. Perhaps that had happened, considering everyone on the ranch but Marcus seemed to have seen these beings. Did Melvin Cunningham really spearhead a coup against members of their own species?

He stared down at Heather's peaceful body resting in the grass. Had she been held against her will? Had all the women who'd come here? So many questions he wouldn't find answers to without shifting.

For the first time, it occurred to him he might not have a choice. Refuge on this ranch could no longer be his only goal. He needed to tell the Spencers what he knew.

The idea twelve women had been kidnapped from their mates and held against their will at the Spencer ranch as his grandfather had suggested to his mother no longer seemed like a viable possibility in any way, as he'd suspected. Marcus believed the women were snatched simultaneously all over the country, but he doubted they'd been previously living in any situation that involved their own free will.

There was no way for Marcus to trust anything he'd heard his grandfather say that day. The man had said enough to make Marcus cringe.

However, what now stood out the most of all the things he'd overheard was the idea the women had been kidnapped from their *mates*. Heather Peters had not been mated. She was his. If she'd been mated to another wolf, two things would have happened. He would be able to smell her unavailability on her, and his body would not recognize an alignment with hers.

Mated couples, even those who met and fell for each other without the assistance of Fate, did not remain available to others. Their scent changed. Their hormones aligned with their mate's, and they were literally and figuratively off the market. Even if there was someone out there who would have belonged to them as their true mate, they would never recognize it.

That was one of the many beauties of their species. Fate had a hand in the entire glorious process.

Heather stilled, and Marcus realized she'd gone to sleep. She rolled toward him, her tail no longer wagging, her jaw open in rest. That she trusted him to watch over her while she healed meant the world to him. She would mend.

Now the only thing left to do was for Marcus to get over himself and take a risk. It would be the biggest risk of his life, but he owed it to the Spencers and perhaps his entire species. He feared the increased intensity of the mating call that would surely amp up his desire for this woman in human form. Facing her and telling her about his past made him wince. Imagining the look of distaste on her face when she found out who he was made his mouth dry and his stomach ache. Her rightful rejection would kill him. He wasn't ready.

CHAPTER 4

Marcus jerked his head up from the floor when he heard the distinct piercing cry of a baby. His mate lay on the couch next to him, her foot propped up. After their romp in the woods earlier, it was swollen, but the redness had gone down.

The back door opened, and the volume of the crying increased tenfold.

"Bring him here," Heather said.

A woman stepped farther into the house.

Marcus couldn't see her face clearly until after she leaned over and handed the baby to Heather. Instantly the baby stopped wailing. *Huh*. Seemed his mate had secret powers, he mused.

He sat up straighter to see the newcomer.

She stared down at him bemused, her mouth quirked on one side. His eyes widened. It was Mackenzie Davis. Obviously this was the woman Heather referred to as Kenzie earlier. Drake's mate. And the very woman Marcus first approached at his grandfather's urging last year at The Gathering. He'd seen her from afar in the last few days, but up close and personal like this, he wanted to swallow his tongue.

He stepped back a pace. Shit. Not that she would recognize him in wolf form.

"So, this is the mysterious black wolf."

"Yep. Isn't he the perfect mate?" Heather chuckled as she jostled the baby on her lap. "He doesn't argue with me. He doesn't take up much space. He's a supreme body guard. Of course the sex isn't what I had expected, but I've got batteries. Who needs it?" She shrugged.

Marcus narrowed his eyes at her. How could she refer to him so flippantly? *She's goading you. Ignore it.*

His gaze wandered back to Mackenzie, who flopped onto the couch when Heather sat up straighter. "That's a shame. You're so good with kids." She stared at Marcus while she spoke. "I'd hate to think you won't have any. Vibrators are wonderful. Don't get me wrong. But they can't impregnate you." She tickled the little guy on Heather's lap.

The baby gurgled. Almost a giggle.

"How do you always manage to accomplish in two seconds what no one else can do in hours?" Kenzie asked.

"What?" Heather laughed. "He likes me."

Marcus closed his eyes as he listened to her laugh. He loved the sound of it. And it broke through this ridiculous talk of vibrators and batteries.

Shaking the visual from his head, he stared at Kenzie. He needed to shift. And the timetable for that had taken a drastic shift with the arrival of one of the women he'd accosted at the last Gathering. He owed her that. Wallowing around in wolf form, not man enough to apologize for his behavior was beneath him. He prayed her sister wasn't around. He couldn't face them both at once.

Groaning, Marcus set his head back down on the ground. He had even more explaining to do now. And the clock was ticking. He needed to shift and take his mate in his arms so badly his skin tingled. The drive hovered beneath his skin, threatening to force him to shift. Not that he would snatch her up and claim her by any stretch of the imagination. He owed her even more explanations than Kenzie. *Again, man up, wolfboy*. He borrowed Heather's term for himself in his mind as he tried to slow his heart rate.

The back door opened again, and Drake walked in.

He shook his head as he stared at Marcus. "The infamous black wolf is still not talking." He propped his hands on his hips as Marcus sat up straight again. "You've met my mate, Kenzie, and our son Aaron, I see. So nice chatting with you." He snickered and took a seat across from the women.

Drake turned to the women. "Dad's on his way in. He has some results from the blood test."

Marcus's ears perked up. Just knowing the outcome would go a long way.

The screen door slammed again, and Jerome entered with Natalie. "Ah, you're all here." He held up a piece of paper as he approached Marcus and then sat on the coffee table in front of him. He looked at Marcus directly as he spoke, which was impressive, respectful, considering Marcus was in wolf form. He was still a human under the furry exterior. And Jerome knew it.

Marcus's heart beat wildly with the stress. He wanted to know what was in the bloodwork at least as much as anyone else in the room.

"There are no traces of drugs in your system. I'd venture to guess if you were drugged, it's been a while since you were last injected. You're completely free of any foreign substance. We can't know for sure if you received Rohypnol or scopolamine because they would have flushed out of your body quickly, especially in wolf form."

Marcus cocked his head, unsure what those drugs were.

Jerome continued. "Those were the drugs the women we rescued had been given. Kinda similar to date-rape drugs."

Marcus's eyes widened. *Something that would make me want to take a woman against her will?* It would explain a lot.

"I've sent the blood off to another location for more testing. There's still the possibility your genetic makeup has been tampered with. Were you aware of that?"

Marcus shook his head. He doubted that was the case since it had been over six years since he'd been used as a guinea pig. Though from listening to his grandfather, he knew other men had been subjected to such testing.

"Huh. Well, I can't see any particular reason why you can't shift. So I'm guessing you have your motives." Jerome stood. "You can stay here. We would never turn away someone's mate. But please seriously consider the long-term ramifications of remaining in such close proximity to your mate without claiming her. It has to be hard on you, but not nearly as difficult as Heather in human form. If you can't or won't shift, I suggest you leave her to move on with her life. This is no way to live."

A hand landed on Marcus's back and dug into his fur. He glanced back at Heather. Tears filled her eyes but refused to spill down her cheeks. She wiped them away with the back of her other hand.

His throat clogged. He couldn't stand it another minute. Even though he may have to suffer the wrath of several people, he needed to shift for his mate's sake.

He stood and nudged Heather's good leg. No way was he going to shift here in the living room. He wanted to be alone with his mate when he met her for the first time. God and everyone didn't need to be present.

His mate stood also. "Listen, mutt, I hope you're ready to reveal yourself. I'm exhausted from the one-way conversations." She limped from the room, her leg much stronger than earlier in the day.

Marcus followed on her heels. When she entered the room he'd first met her in, still convinced it wasn't strictly her room, she shut the door behind them. She hobbled over to the bed and climbed into the center, crossing her legs beneath her. She narrowed her gaze at him.

He thought about shifting right there and then. But he couldn't imagine how he might look without a shower and a comb. Instead, he turned from her and headed toward the bathroom, nudging the door open and pushing his way into the small space. He turned to look back at her before shutting the door.

She nodded and smiled, encouraging him to go on.

Marcus nosed the door shut with a resounding click.

Even though it had been weeks since he last shifted, in moments he was standing in her bathroom in human form staring down at himself. Thank God he'd gone with this option. He was dirty, and his hair was a mess. He flipped on the shower and stepped in before it warmed up.

He set his hands on the tile wall and let the water sluice over him. He tried to catch his breath.

The trouble was this room was filled with the scent of his mate, and the moment he'd shifted and taken his human form, he'd been slammed with her smell permeating the air. His cock jumped to attention. He hadn't had sex in a long time with any woman, but never had he been this instantly aroused.

Holy shit. He closed his eyes and took his dick in his hand. If he didn't bring himself to a quick orgasm before he left this bathroom, he wasn't sure he could control himself after exiting.

I'm not sure I can control myself even after getting off in the shower.

He did it anyway. A few quick thrusts and he shot his come against the wall. His breathing increased until he was panting. And every breath he took drew more and more of his sweet mate into his system.

This was nothing like the lust he'd felt toward Mackenzie or her sister at The Gathering just over a year ago. His grandfather had steered him very much astray. Intentionally. Why? He wanted to slam his fist into the wall, but it would solve nothing. And besides, his first order of business was confronting the woman who indeed was his mate. He'd deal with the rest after.

∼

"Are you going to stay in there all day?" Heather squirmed against the mattress where she sat, restless. Impatient.

She knew he was finally in human form. Besides the shower and the rummaging around she could hear, she'd sensed him the moment he'd shifted. Even through the closed door she could smell his personal musk, and she was anxious to meet him.

He didn't respond. She could hear the toilet flush, the sink run, and the distinct sound of him brushing his teeth. It made her smile. Was he using her toothbrush?

She glanced down at herself. Maybe she should have dressed nicer. In jean shorts and a tank top, she was very ordinary today. Self-consciousness seeped into her skin. Goose bumps rose in its wake.

She rubbed her arms, crossing them in front of her.

Maybe he had some sort of deformity he didn't want her to see. No. That wasn't likely. She'd have seen evidence in his wolf form. A scar, though. That would have been covered with his fur.

She didn't have to wait any longer. She flinched as the door opened and lifted her gaze.

Heather froze. She held her breath to control her reaction.

Whether her initial reaction was caused by Fate or lust or her secret inner desires, the man who emerged from the bathroom took her breath away.

Her mouth fell open. His expression was serious as he approached, his brow furrowed. He was deeply tanned in stark contrast to her own pale skin. His chest bulged with muscles. He wore nothing more than a towel wrapped around his waist, low and precarious.

She wished it would fall.

She lifted her gaze to his face again. Dark hair, almost black, slicked back from his forehead. He'd combed it, but it was wet. Probably in need of a cut. But right then all she could think of was weaving her fingers into it. Would it fall across his brow when it dried?

His eyes penetrated hers. Deep chocolate, as she'd seen in his wolf form.

He stopped midway across the room and stared at her for long moments.

Heather sat up straighter, gripping her knees with both hands to avoid flinging herself at him. Never had she been so drawn to another human being. Her entire body went on full alert in reaction to his presence only feet away from her. In human form his pheromones brought the mating instinct closer to the surface. She needed him to claim her right now.

Why wasn't he moving?

A deep inhale caused her to breathe in more of his scent until she grew dizzy with lust.

She licked her lips. "You don't talk any more in human form than in wolf form."

The dark man lifted his gaze from perusing her body to meet her eyes. He smiled...more like half smiled. "Marcus."

Marcus. She rolled the name around in her head. It suited him. Better than wolfboy or mutt, anyway.

She couldn't hold still and found herself squirming around until she was on all fours, climbing across the mattress in his direction. "Are you just going to stand there?"

Marcus stepped back a pace, shocking her. He groaned and rolled his head toward the ceiling, swiping a hand down his face. "Stop that. You're distracting me."

She froze, glancing down at her body to realize what a sultry pose she'd assumed en route to her mate. She didn't drop the position, however. Let him suffer.

"We need to talk."

She lifted her gaze back to meet his. "We do. This is true. How about later?" Whatever the hell possessed her to be so bold, her cheeks flamed at the internal admission. She swallowed and shook the insanity from her head, trying to come up with something to say that wouldn't make her sound so...needy. "I mean, there are so many things I want to know about you, but it won't change the facts."

"It might." He stiffened, his eyes furrowing as he watched her.

Heather flinched. She swiveled around and sat on the edge of the bed. Why was this so difficult? She'd never met a man in her life who would turn down such a blatant offer for sex. Was this man not as attracted to her as she was to him? Surely fate wouldn't fuck up something as important as this.

Her shoulders slumped as she exhaled, biting her bottom lip between her teeth.

"Heather, there are things you need to know. I can't claim you. It would be insensitive."

"What?" she nearly shouted the word before she could rein it in. She closed her eyes, fighting the urge to scream in frustration. "Is this a one-way street?" she whispered.

"A one-way street? Oh. Hell no. Baby, I'm as attracted to you as you are to me. More so, I'm sure."

"Really?" She opened her eyes, narrowing her gaze on him. Sarcasm oozed out with the one word. "Because I'm thinking you must be mistaken. If you were half as interested in claiming me as what I'm feeling, you wouldn't be standing so far away staring at me as though I were a piranha." That wasn't entirely true. His look projected frustration more than anything else.

Marcus cleared his throat. "I'm not some random shifter who happened upon you in that field, baby. I was there on purpose. I came to talk to the Spencers. Encountering you wasn't on the agenda."

She flinched and then scooted back on the bed to put a bit more space between them. Obviously he wasn't consumed with the same lust slamming into her. Her heart beat so loud, she thought he might be able to hear it.

He stepped forward. "That didn't come out quite right." He ran a hand through his hair, disheveling it more than it already was and making her fight against moaning at the sexy look he unintentionally brought on.

Damn him. In addition to lust, she now felt a certain level of anger. And what was worse was it didn't dampen the desire. The only saving grace so far in this conversation was the endearing way he kept calling her "baby" as though she truly did mean more to him than his stance and reluctance would indicate.

Marcus continued. "I've done some things I'm not proud of."

"Haven't we all?"

"Perhaps, but I think I win this time." He took another step toward her. "You deserve to know more about me before you commit to me for life."

At least he wasn't discounting the idea of claiming her. She couldn't imagine what he could say to dissuade her.

Another deep breath from Marcus. "My name is Marcus Cunningham."

So?

"Does that ring a bell?"

She shook her head.

"My grandfather is Melvin Cunningham. He's a member of The Head Council."

"Oh. Right. Of course." What was he trying to say? That he was too good for her?

"He's the leader of this estranged group that calls themselves the Romulus."

Her eyes shot open wide. She scrambled backward

now, putting more space between herself and Marcus. Perhaps Fate really had fucked up this time.

"See? Now do you understand the need for conversation? Or did you still want me to claim you right this second?"

She didn't move an inch. Her breath was shallow. Fear ate a hole in her. If she screamed, would the Spencers still be in the other room to hear her?

He held out a hand. "I'm not going to hurt you, Heather. Ever. As of yesterday, you're the most important person in my life, and I would never do anything to jeopardize that. But you deserve to make your own choices, and mating with me might not be on your short list. I assume it won't. But I'm not a big enough asshole not to acknowledge that and provide you with the option to beg out."

Heather didn't move a muscle. She tried not to breathe deeply. Every time she did, his scent scrambled her brain. Her damn body didn't give a hoot who he was or what he might have done. It wanted him anyway. Her belly was tight with arousal.

"To avoid redundancy, it would be best if I spoke to the Spencers at the same time as you. They need to hear everything I have to say also."

She nodded, both relieved he wasn't going to pounce on her and aggravated they needed to leave the room and face other people without mating. Was he a member of the Romulus himself? Why wasn't he a superwolf?

Marcus turned toward the door to the bedroom and opened it. A second later, he reached down to grab something and spun back around. "The Spencers are good people, aren't they?" he asked, holding up a pile of clothes.

Heather nodded again. "The best." Of course they would leave him something to wear outside the door.

Marcus ducked back into the bathroom and returned moments later wearing loose jeans and a T-shirt. Not perfect fitting, but close.

She tried not to groan over the fact he was no longer nearly naked, his delicious chest now covered with cotton.

God, please don't ruin my life by aligning me with the enemy...

∽

Marcus held her gaze as he stepped toward the door again. He reached out a hand and then dropped it just as fast, wiping his palm on his jeans. "Sorry, baby. I wish there was another way." He ducked his head. "Come."

The second he opened the door this time, he heard voices. The Spencers were waiting. Not surprising.

Heather followed behind, but not close enough to touch him. He couldn't blame her.

"Oh good. You're human," Drake teased, the first to speak. His face fell immediately however.

Naturally. Marcus imagined the look on his face was enough to sober everyone.

"I'm Drake." He extended a hand, his smile gone, replaced by a serious furrow of his brow.

"Marcus."

Jerome stood. "Welcome." He and Natalie came in from the kitchen area of the great room and sat on a love seat. "Please, sit." He motioned toward the couch.

Marcus sat on the couch where Jerome indicated, but Heather didn't sit next to him. Instead she chose an armchair nearby. Marcus waited for Scott to grab a seat. He figured Scott was about twenty-four. Drake was closer to thirty. And Marcus knew there was another son missing who fell between them in age.

Jerrod was no longer in the great room. Neither was Kenzie. Relief gave Marcus the courage to continue. At least he didn't have to tell his tale in front of a young teen or the woman who would immediately recognize him from last year.

"First of all," Marcus began, "let me thank you for taking me in, especially under the strange circumstances. I admit I have been wandering your property for several days trying to figure out a way to approach." He glanced at his mate. "Heather ended that pretty quickly." He glanced at her and then back at Jerome. Just having Heather in the room was a challenge. He needed her like he'd never craved anything in his life. It took every ounce of his strength to face these people first and let Heather decide if she was willing to give him a chance.

Before shifting, he'd envisioned Heather running from the room and never looking back. Now, however, he prayed to every imaginable god she might be able to give him a chance. That was how much stronger the mating call slammed into him once he was in human form.

"You're welcome." Jerome nodded. His brow was furrowed. "What brought you here?"

"Refuge, initially. I didn't know where else to go. I don't know how much of what I have to say you already know, but I suspect not all of it. And I'm sure you can shed light on several questions I have too. I'm very concerned about the direction of the shifter population."

"As are we," Jerome said. "It's a mess, for sure."

"Let me start by telling you my last name."

Scott leaned forward. "What is it?"

"Cunningham." He waited for his surname to sink in.

"As in Melvin Cunningham?" Natalie asked.

"The very one, yes. Do you know him?"

"Not personally," she began, "but I've met him a few times. I know he's one of the five Head Council elders."

"Yes. He's my grandfather. Though I'd hesitate to claim him as a blood relative these days."

Jerome gasped. He leaned forward. "I didn't realize he had a son?"

"He doesn't. He has a daughter. My mother, Lora. But since she's his only child and my father is a bit… well, let's just say, he's Granddad's lackey, he took the name Cunningham when they married."

Jerome furrowed his brow. "Okaaay. Go on."

"The man has not been a good influence on me, that's for sure." Marcus glanced at everyone in the room as he spoke, gauging their reactions. So far no one was judging him. They all took his information in stride. Even Heather, whom he didn't make eye contact with for fear he wouldn't be able to continue.

"I'm not going to sugarcoat this. The man is a vile excuse for a living being. He pumped me full of drugs for years in my youth, telling my parents it was for my own good, that he was trying to bulk me up. That I was too skinny." Marcus licked his lips, wishing he had a glass of water. Bile rose in his throat at the thought of his grandfather.

He continued. "When I was about nineteen, I started faking it, hiding the pills anywhere I could and not taking his weird concoctions. I know now he was using me for his experiments, like a guinea pig."

Heather gasped.

"As soon as my head cleared, I was able to figure out my grandfather was a quack. At least that's what I assumed at the time. He seemed harmless enough. Just some old guy who thought I needed steroids or something. I took control of my own life, joined a gym, and got stronger on my own. I'm sure nature had a hand in it also."

"How old are you now?" Jerome asked.

"Twenty-six."

"So it's been over six years since you were under the influence of his drugs?" Marcus could tell Jerome fought hard to keep from leaping up and pacing the room in frustration, and he appreciated the sentiment. It was more than he'd ever gotten from his own father.

"With the exception of one other incident, yes. But I'll come back to that." He glanced at Drake, hating what he needed to tell the man. "I moved out of my parents' home when I was twenty, got a job in construction, and assumed a normal life. At least until about a month ago."

Jerome nodded. He didn't interrupt. Everyone else sat very still. They must have been shocked. Marcus couldn't blame them.

"I've always been in contact with my parents, especially my mother. My father, Carl, tends to think like my grandfather. Nevertheless, I ignored their idiosyncrasies most of my adult life. So, that particular Sunday afternoon I headed to my parents' home for dinner and arrived in time to overhear them talking to my grandfather in the living room. Instead of entering the house, I eavesdropped from the porch and got an earful I'll never forget."

"I'll bet. This is huge. Do you know that?" Jerome asked.

"I assumed."

"So, Cunningham is the mole everyone's been looking for within The Head Council."

"Yes. I'm sure he is. The man runs that secret organization called the Romulus."

When everyone nodded, he went on. They all knew about the Romulus. Probably far more than he knew.

"He's grooming ordinary shifters to become some kind of superwolves."

Jerome cocked one eyebrow. "He's way past that, son. He's been abundantly successful."

Marcus nodded. "I gathered that when you all mentioned superwolves this morning. I assume you've seen them?"

Jerome shook his head. "Son, we've fought against them on this ranch."

"I figured. Anyway, my grandfather's goal that

particular Sunday was to convince my mother he needed to bring me into the fold. I'm his only heir. He specifically mentioned some new research that would alter my genes and make me part of his army."

Drake gasped. "I wonder if he's found a way to alter shifters who don't have the correct gene sequence. Did you get the impression he already had the capability?"

"Not sure, but he did say he had the financial backing of someone very wealthy, and he intended to use the man's money to build his army and in return provide the manpower to do whatever the guy needed. It scared the fuck out of me."

"How did you find us?"

"My grandfather told my parents that your family was harboring women who had been kidnapped from their mates."

Jerome scowled. "You're shitting me. That bastard. Those Romulus assholes were the ones who did the kidnapping. NAR went in to rescue those women, none of whom were mated."

"Yeah, I gathered that. That's why I came here. Took me a while, and when I arrived, I spent several days hanging back watching to make sure I hadn't misjudged you." Marcus glanced at Heather. Her eyes were huge saucers, and her mouth was open.

"Shit." Jerome stood now. He ran a hand through his hair. "I need to call Jerard."

"Yeah, I'm sure you do. That's the most important part I know. But there's more. You make your call first. I'm sure Jerard needs to know posthaste. The rest is personal."

Everyone waited while Jerome place the call to Jerard and then repeated the information to someone named Evan and another guy named Daniel who Marcus realized was the Spencers' other son and a member of NAR.

The most important thing Marcus learned from listening to Jerome's half of the conversation was although many wolves had been transformed into superwolves, apparently not all shifters had the gene that permitted the transformation. Marcus shivered when he realized his grandfather had been speaking of altering Marcus's own DNA to allow for the change.

When Jerome finally hung up, he was restless.

Natalie spoke first. "Was he shocked?"

"In a sense. But he knew there was a mole, and he'd suspected Cunningham for a while. The man is odd, let's just say."

"Would someone mind filling me in on what really happened with the kidnapped women?" Marcus asked. "I'm confused about the sequence of events."

Jerome spoke. "Twelve women had been kidnapped by the Romulus and taken to remote locations. They were injected with various drugs, or in some cases given pills. One other woman, Ashley, was rescued after four years of captivity. That was a year ago, long before this latest mission. She was the first to be recovered. Her mate, Evan—"

"Wait. She was mated?"

"Well, not until after she was rescued. In fact Evan was the private investigator hired by her family to find her. She lives with him in St. Louis now."

"God." Marcus gripped his thighs as he listened to the unbelievable tale.

"Anyway," Jerome continued, "Evan was hired by Jerard to find other missing women. He organized a sting, and all twelve were rescued at the same time. They were brought here over the next few days when we offered our ranch as a refuge for them to recover and get the counseling they needed. They reunited with their families here."

Marcus looked at Heather. "You were one of those women, weren't you?"

She nodded.

"Shit. My grandfather is quite a piece of work. No wonder I was confused. He said the women were all happily mated living normal lives until The Head Council kidnapped them." He shook his head. "I knew for a fact something was out of whack when I realized Heather wasn't mated to someone else. In fact, I don't even think my parents know the true story behind it all. They seem only privileged to whatever info my grandfather has fed them. And most of what he says is lies."

"It's an enormous disaster, for sure." Jerome paced again as he spoke. "So, in a nutshell, the women came here, we figured out half of them had GPS tracking devices imbedded in their necks, removed the chips, and then had to move them to other safe houses. It's unfortunate. We'd hoped they could stay here and recover. But it wasn't safe.

"In fact, NAR descended on us to provide protection, and we ended up in a small war against the unbelievable Romulus right here on our property. You will be very shocked when you see the results of your grandfather's little project. Somehow he has tampered with their DNA and produced an entire army of superwolves. They're huge, and they're strong. They also heal faster than ordinary wolves."

Marcus was stunned. "And now my grandfather has apparently bumped that up a step and found a way to transform even those shifters who don't have the correct DNA sequence to become superwolves. That must have been what he intended to do to me."

Jerome nodded. "Sounds that way."

Marcus turned to his mate. "You stayed here on the ranch."

She nodded. "I didn't want to go back to my family in Oregon. They live in a small town. It gave me the willies all my life. After I was kidnapped, I never wanted to return. The Spencers were gracious enough to offer me a home until I could get my feet under me. I have a degree in nursing. I've been applying around the country…and then you showed up." She tipped her head to one side, but her expression was unreadable.

Marcus didn't want to burden her by asking about her kidnapping experience right then, but he would want the details later. Even though her tale might make him vomit, or decide to personally kill his own flesh and blood.

He turned to Jerome. "Where's your other son? Daniel, right?"

"Yes. One of the rescued women, Allison, turned out to be his mate. She's of some unknown importance to the Romulus. Daniel is a member of NAR. They're in Seattle where both The Head Council and the main military hub is located. Well, maybe they are. Allison is in a safe house. It could be anywhere."

Marcus ran a hand through his hair. "I can't wrap my mind around all this."

"Neither can we," Jerome said. "But bless you for coming here and providing us with the most valuable breakthrough we've had yet."

"You're welcome, of course." Marcus had an idea. "Oh my God. I have to go back." He jumped from his seat.

"What are you talking about? Go back where?" Heather asked.

Marcus looked at Jerome, meeting his gaze eye to eye as the man realized his meaning. He shook his head. "No one would ask that of you."

"No one *did*. But you know it's the only way."

"What?" Heather stood now and stepped forward. "Someone please tell me what you're talking about." Her voice rose to a new level.

Drake cleared his throat. "He means he's going to go undercover. As a spy."

"*No*," Heather screamed. She jerked her gaze up, her eyes wide with fear. She shook her head. "You can't. You just got here." She shook.

Marcus smiled at her, extremely relieved by her vehemence concerning him. It was the first indication he had that she might be able to move forward with him even though he was related to the enemy. Of course there was more she didn't know. And some of it was almost worse. But this couldn't be helped. "I know, baby. But this is important. The survival of our species could depend on my ability to infiltrate the Romulus and stop them from ruining our way of life."

She still shook her head. "No. Someone else can do it."

"There's no one else."

She shook, her entire body quivering. She wrapped her arms around her middle and hugged herself. Marcus wanted to go to her and hold her. But he couldn't. Not yet.

"Let's not get carried away," Jerome said. "No one's going anywhere right this minute. It will take a few days to plan. We'd need to meet with several people. The Head Council would want to gather and fill Marcus in on everything. Don't panic yet. But Marcus is right. The plan might be our best shot. Did you say your grandfather had come to your parents' house to bring you into the fold?"

"Yes." Marcus nodded. "That's precisely why this will work. I'll go back, let them bring me in, and then gather all the information I can." Marcus met Heather's gaze as she pursed her lips, no longer protesting, at least not out loud.

He took a deep breath. "There's one more thing I have to tell you." He turned toward Drake. "And it concerns you."

"Me?" Drake pointed at himself.

Everyone calmed down and quieted.

"I told you there was one instance when I was

drugged in the last six years. I need to explain that day, and you aren't going to like it." Marcus kept his gaze locked on Drake's. "It was at The Gathering last year. My grandfather nagged me to find a mate. I don't know what his motives were yet, nor do I understand why he picked the particular women he chose, but he injected me with some mind-altering drug. He caught me off guard and stabbed me with a needle so fast I couldn't stop him.

"And then he proceeded to brainwash me, filling my head with all sorts of crazy ideas. He kept insisting I find a mate. I grew more confused under the influence of the drug as the weekend wore on."

Drake gasped. He gripped the arms of his chair, but he didn't interrupt.

Marcus saw the moment Drake knew where this story was going, but he continued. He needed to say everything out loud. And he needed everyone in the room to have a fair opportunity to assess his behavior.

Including Heather. Especially Heather. Whatever future Marcus may have with her hinged on this information and her ability to overlook his transgressions. He couldn't imagine how she could continue to make eye contact with him after she heard the rest. "Eventually he convinced me one particular woman was destined to be mine. I didn't give it much thought. I had only one thing on my mind as I approached her, and that was getting laid."

Heather flinched. And she should. There was no use sugarcoating it.

"It's true. I guess the drug was some sort of

aphrodisiac. I couldn't seem to stop myself from taking what my grandfather said was mine."

"Kenzie." The one word came out of Drake's mouth on a sigh.

Marcus nodded. "And then her sister, Kathleen." He paused. "I'm terribly sorry for the trauma I caused your mate and her sister. I don't expect either of them to forgive me, but that day has haunted me for fifteen months. I want to personally apologize for my behavior."

Drake nodded. Silence ensued for several heartbeats.

Drake finally spoke again. "My mate is not the type to harbor a grudge. Even when she told me about you later that day, she insinuated you weren't in your right mind. She was shook up from your attempted advances, but she didn't suffer long. I came along and wiped you from her memory." He smiled.

Marcus's chest pounded. How could this man be so kind about what Marcus had done to his mate?

"You didn't mean it." He glanced toward the soft voice of his own mate. Her eyes were glazed with tears, but he realized she was crying with him, not about him. She hurt for the man who'd been drugged and brainwashed. She wasn't angry. She didn't hate him. A long exhale escaped his lips. "I need a moment."

Marcus left the room to step out the front door and gasp for oxygen. Even in the late evening, the air was too warm, suffocating him. He bent at the waist, afraid he would hyperventilate. Setting his hands on his knees, he dipped his head and tried to breathe normally.

Soft hands wrapped around him from behind. He

smelled his mate before he saw her. Somehow she'd followed him without him hearing the door. Or maybe he'd never shut it behind him. He'd been so hell-bent on gasping for breath.

Her tiny hands grasped him around the waist, and she leaned in to lay her face on his back. "I'm so sorry that happened to you," she whispered. "It's unconscionable what your grandfather did. I hope I never make his acquaintance. But no one here is going to blame you for actions beyond your control." She held him for long minutes.

Finally Marcus managed to turn in her arms and wrap his hands around her, pressing her head to his chest and burying his face in her hair. He breathed her floral-scented shampoo deep into his lungs.

He was one lucky bastard. She smelled like heaven, and having her in his arms was a dream.

∽

Heather held on to her mate for long minutes, not willing to let go for a second. Now that she'd finally touched him, she couldn't break the contact for anything in the world.

But they were on the front porch. Not a good place to fuck. "Let's go back inside. We need some time alone." She lifted her gaze to meet his, feeling the grip of his hand buried in her hair.

He nodded and held her against his side as they reentered the house and made their way toward the bedroom she'd been using for several weeks. The

Spencers had gone out the back apparently. The house was quiet.

Heather wasn't surprised. Obviously Heather and Marcus had a lot to consider privately.

Marcus shut the bedroom door behind him and leaned against it. Immediately Heather felt a heightened awareness of his presence in the confined space, a room he'd already filled with his scent in both human and wolf form. Her entire body tingled as it came alive.

He held her at arm's length and met her gaze, his expression serious. "I don't expect you to let me claim you."

"I expect you to stop talking and get on with it." She grinned, batting her eyes playfully.

"Heather..." Marcus rolled his eyes. "This is serious. I'm a blood relative of the man running this crazy attempt to ruin all that we have worked for centuries to maintain as a species."

She opened her mouth to protest, but Marcus set a finger on her lips.

"Baby, listen to me."

Her toes curled when he called her that. A shiver raced up her spine, and she gripped his biceps where he held on to her shoulders.

"I've not always been drug free. I don't even know what's been in my system."

"Whatever it was, it's not there now. It's not controlling you, Marcus, and you know it."

He hesitated. "I nearly forced myself on Mackenzie, and she lives on this ranch."

"You can't be held accountable for that."

Marcus opened his mouth but appeared to be out of arguments.

Heather was glad. She leaned forward, in part to stop him from saying more, but also because her body swayed in his direction of its own accord. She needed to kiss him. Taste him. Know the feel of his lips on hers.

But Marcus had other ideas. He righted himself and backed her up until she hit the bed. He sat her down and kneeled in front of her, bringing his face level with hers. He stared at her long moments, a smile forming on the corners of his mouth. "Am I really this lucky?"

She couldn't speak. But he didn't continue, either. It didn't matter. Words were superfluous at the moment.

Finally he set both hands on her knees and trailed them up her thighs.

Heather gasped as she gripped his shoulders.

"Are you sure?"

"Never been more positive."

He continued up her waist until he held her beneath her chest, his thumbs grazing the undersides of her breasts. He stood, leaning closer. He eased her onto her back, scooting her farther across the mattress with his grip and climbing over her at the same time.

When he lowered his body onto her, she let out a long moan, unable to stop it, instantly feeling the flames creep up her cheeks at her reaction.

His smile widened as he nestled between her legs and lowered his lips to hers.

Slowly. So slowly he advanced. Too damn slow.

She licked her dry mouth, her gaze following his plump lips as they reached her, and he finally closed the distance. The kiss was tentative at first. One hand trailed up her body and held her face, causing her to meet his gaze.

Their eyes met, and she blinked. God, how she wanted him. Needed him with every fiber of her being. She didn't care about his past or her own, as long as he claimed her right here, right now. Her pussy clenched, desperate against the rigid length of his cock nestled over her clit.

And then he tipped his head and took the kiss deeper, his tongue darting out to meet hers. He licked her lips and devoured her with the kiss. A deep moan escaped his mouth as he gripped her tighter, one hand still on her side beneath her breast and the other stroking her cheek.

Her breath hitched when his chest lowered farther, making her hyper-aware of her nipples as they beaded against the lace of her bra.

Nothing could have prepared her for the onslaught of emotion consuming her, threatening to overpower her and suck the air out of her lungs.

One second he'd been hesitant and concerned—the next he'd switched to controlled and urgent. He held her tighter, his lips demanding and firm against hers.

Heather grabbed his waist with both hands, her fingers slipping under his T-shirt to graze his skin. His clothes could disappear into the ether for all she cared. She wanted to see all of him.

He was impressively the sexiest man alive with his dark, brooding looks and intense gaze. For all she had toyed with him as though he were a stray mutt, he scrambled her brain so completely with his virility she couldn't think straight.

She shouldn't be surprised, really. He'd been nothing but growly and protective since she'd met him. Plus he was a wolf. His alpha tendencies were sexy and attractive. Not off-putting in the least. She wanted him to take her—any way he pleased. As long as it was now.

Heather was a strong woman. Never had she let herself be so consumed. Usually she felt completely in control of her surroundings. She'd been able to control even the largest man in the hospital when finishing nursing school. She considered herself an Alpha of the female version. She made up for her small stature in personality.

Now all that shattered. And she didn't care.

Marcus pulled his mouth back and set his forehead against hers. "You're mine."

She nodded, biting her lower lip. Wetness flooded her pussy as he spoke those two words. His voice was deep, deeper than it had been before he was consumed with lust, but his tone sent a shiver down her spine and made her squirm beneath him, longing to hear more.

He lowered his hand from her face, holding her gaze, and grazed it down her body until he reached the hem of her shirt. When he wiggled his fingers under the tight cotton, Heather gasped. His firm hand splayed over her belly, caressing her skin, bringing forth goose bumps in its wake.

Whatever he had in mind, she was helpless to protest. In fact, she bucked her hips toward him to gain more purchase against his cock.

He lowered his hand and held her hip down. "Still."

One word.

Her chest pounded. Her cheeks burned. She was so aroused.

Her mate released her hip and lifted his chest off her enough to push her shirt up her body with his hand. She felt the exaggerated rise and fall of her chest as he exposed her bra.

He glanced down at the lace and leaned to one side to give himself better access. With one finger, he traced the center edge of her bra, so lightly she could barely feel the touch. But she knew he was there. His gaze was focused on her breasts while she watched the intensity in his furrowed forehead.

When he dipped a finger under the lace and flicked it over her nipple, she bucked. Her pussy throbbed with need, a ball forming in the pit of her stomach, threatening to explode.

She swallowed past the arousal building in her entire body. Growing.

Her mate was no stray mutt…

He continued to circle her breast with his finger. He tugged the cup down, forcing her breast up high and firm. And then he dipped his head and took her nipple into his mouth.

Heather released his hips and gripped the bedding on both sides of her. She tipped her neck back to breathe air not quite so concentrated with his scent. It didn't work.

She gasped for oxygen when he gripped her breast with his hand and sucked deeper. Fearing she might come any second, she lay very still. If he so much as budged against her clit, she would come.

Butterflies flipped in her belly. They seemed to flap against her insides, vying for escape.

With expert hands, her mate popped the center clasp on her bra, exposing her completely to his gaze. He'd seen her in a tank top, but this was so much more intimate.

She felt exposed like never before.

With obvious intent, he lifted off her body, shoved her shirt and bra over her head, and released them. He met her gaze as he popped the button on her shorts and then lowered the zipper. He inhaled long and slow as her arousal filled the air. She could smell her need. "Please," she mumbled. She reached for him, but her fingers were useless.

With a grin, Marcus lifted his own shirt over his head and tossed it aside also.

Quickly he straddled her legs and tugged her shorts down, taking her panties with them. Both items fell to the floor as he nudged her legs apart and kneeled between them.

Heather's chest rose and fell, even though her breathing seemed very shallow.

His gaze roamed over her body, his fingers trailing in the same spots.

She lifted her head to look down. So wanton. Her nipples stood at attention. Her breasts ached, seeming much larger than ever before.

No man she'd ever dated made her feel this beautiful. Worshipped.

Her mate stroked her skin, intent on touching every inch of her.

She gripped the blankets again, tighter this time.

Dark eyes met hers. He paused, his gaze penetrating.

He lowered his face again to peruse her body. She hadn't been privy to his yet, but the bulge in his jeans told her there would be an impressive cock under there.

He was as silent in human form as he'd been in wolf form. But he communicated so much more. And he did it well.

When he pushed her legs open wider and tilted his gaze to her pussy, moisture pooled at her entrance. She shouldn't be embarrassed, but she couldn't help it.

He stood from the bed and stared down at her, his only movement his chest rising and falling. He wrapped his hands around her thighs and tugged her toward the edge of the bed.

Heather squeaked as he handled her. There was no place to put her feet this close to the side, but he took care of that easily by wrapping his palms around her thighs, holding her legs open and splayed, and dipping his face in toward her center.

She moaned. Even without any contact, he made her want. Her ears burned. She was crazy with need. So fucking horny she couldn't focus on anything. Her vision clouded. Nothing in her past had ever compared to this. Arousal slammed her entire body until she could think of nothing else but mating.

She squeezed her fists tighter, willing him to do…anything.

He seemed to have four hands the way he held her

so wide and still managed to stroke her with his thumbs. He grazed over her swollen lower lips several times and then pulled them apart and inhaled deeply.

Her mate growled. She lowered her gaze, half expecting to find a wolf. But no. He managed to make such a primal sound in human form. His eyes dipped closed, and he plunged forward, consuming her pussy so fast she gasped. She had to bite her lip to keep from screaming. The last thing she wanted was for the Spencers to hear her.

Her mate thrust his tongue inside her and lapped at her channel as though starving. The second he pressed his lips to her clit, she shot off, her orgasm taking over her entire body. She moaned, all attempts at silence out the window. She bucked her hips and pressed her pussy wantonly into his open mouth. He didn't protest. Instead he expertly worked her through the orgasm, easing away from her sensitive skin at the right moment.

She panted, sweat running down her brow. And she wanted more. She nailed him with her gaze, willed him to climb on top of her and take her completely. Maybe she could express her desire with her eyes without begging.

Finally, he lifted his face, licked his lips, and smiled at her. Without wasting another second, he scooted her back to the center of the mattress, dropped his jeans, and climbed over her. He lodged his cock at her entrance and stilled. She could feel the tip, so close. She never even got to see his dick before he was over her.

He reached for her face, held her chin, and met her gaze, searching with his eyes for something.

Heather swallowed and tried to find her voice. "Claim me."

That was all he needed. He thrust into her to the hilt so fast the air whooshed from her lungs.

Her mate sighed, his teeth gritted. Good. He wasn't as restrained as he projected. He drew her up tight against him, his hands snuggled under her armpits, and pumped in and out of her with slower strokes after the initial thrust. Eventually he met her gaze again and held it while he increased the pace.

Her arousal shot back up in a hurry, the girth of his cock filling her so completely she couldn't help but reach another peak. The base of his cock hit the oversensitized skin surrounding her clit again and again.

As his face drew up, she knew he was getting close. She wrapped her hands around his biceps. Suddenly, her mate released her with one arm and lifted his torso enough to reach between them. He pinched her clit firmly, unexpectedly, forcing her to orgasm again at the same moment he did.

She couldn't see for several seconds. All she could do was feel his thick cock pulsing into her as she gripped it with her channel. Long moments of release ruined her for any other man. She was his now. Mated. Claimed. Completed.

When her mate was finally sated, he collapsed to one side of her, drawing her body with him. They remained face to face on their sides, his cock still imbedded inside her.

He met her gaze and smiled, brushing a lock of hair from her face as he softened.

She fell in love with him at that moment. One fantastic fuck, and she was a goner. "You aren't very wordy when you're in the zone, are you?"

He laughed again. She loved the sound and thanked God he had another side than the serious beast who'd just claimed her. "Maybe I'm a man of few words." He stroked her hair. Another moment of silence, and then he spoke again. "You're gorgeous. Been wanting to tell you that since yesterday." He lowered his gaze from her hair to her face. "And even more beautiful when you come."

She felt the pink as it warmed her cheeks again.

Marcus thumbed her face. "When you embarrass, your pale skin pinkens. It's precious."

"I don't embarrass easily."

He lifted one brow and cocked his mouth.

"Well, except when some wolfboy waltzes in, strips me, and then stares at my…my…"

"Pussy?" He chuckled.

She rolled her eyes. "Are you always so…forward?"

"Yep."

She rolled her eyes again. "Here we are with the wordiness once more."

He tweaked her cheek and eased away from her. "Lie on your belly."

She hesitated.

He rolled his eyes. "You're so tense. I'm going to rub your shoulders."

She melted at the sound of his voice and lowered her

face to the pillow he pulled under her. Her body came to life thinking about him smoothing his hands over her, and she hid her face to keep him from seeing how much more red she surely was.

She was shocked when he climbed over her, straddling her ass, and kneaded his hands into her shoulders. How did he have so much energy after what they just did? She was putty.

"I have a lot of questions still, but I couldn't concentrate on any of them until after I claimed you. My lips wouldn't move."

She knew the feeling.

"After spending almost twenty-four hours with you but unable to touch you intimately… I was a ticking time bomb."

She gripped the sheets alongside her face into fists as his hands worked magic on her back and wetness flooded between her legs again.

He dug his thumbs into just the right spots along her spine and shoulder blades before he spoke again. "I'm not done with you. I need you again."

"Thank God," she muttered into the pillow. Was it just the mating? Or was it more? He seemed to command her body.

He leaned forward and set his lips on her ear, his breath sending a shiver down her spine. "You're so sexy sprawled out like this."

Her shiver turned into a full-body shudder. He squeezed her ass cheeks with both hands and molded them to his palms, and then he slinked back down alongside her, grazing lightly over her skin.

She stared at him. She missed the way he held her down with his body over hers. He was so much more than she'd anticipated when she met him in the woods.

His expression was serious again. "Will you tell me what happened to you?"

She swallowed. "I was kidnapped by the Romulus and drugged."

He squeezed her bicep. "I'm so sorry."

She gave him a weak smile. "It wasn't as bad for me as some of the other women. I was only held a week before NAR rescued me."

"I'm not sure that makes me feel better."

She lifted a hand and stroked his cheek, loving the feeling of his unshaved face. She smiled inside, imagining him deciding he couldn't take the time to shave before he emerged from the bathroom. Day-old growth coated his face. That's probably where it was when he'd shifted. "I'm going to be okay."

He kissed her palm. "I want to hear the rest when you're ready."

She lifted to sitting so she could see him better. "When did you recognize me as your mate? Were you watching me?"

He took her hand and brought it to his lips. "No. Nothing like that. I hadn't been close enough. I saw you collapse in the field, and I couldn't let some woman disappear between the tall grasses and leave her there. I'm more couth than that. I didn't know if you'd fallen into a hole, been caught in a trap, or fainted. I didn't realize you were mine until I got closer. And then my heart beat out of my body to make sure you were alive."

She stared at him. She loved the way he said "you were mine."

Marcus reached with both hands and cupped her breasts. His thumbs worked over her nipples until she moaned.

She tipped her head back. "How can I be this aroused again?" Her voice was soft, barely audible.

"It's the mating, baby." He pinched her nipples between his thumbs and index fingers. "Your skin is so soft."

She shivered as he pulled her down next to him once again and settled her on her back to lean over her.

He shook his head. "Let's table this conversation for later. We could go on for hours. I'd rather spend time right now making sure this claiming sticks before we face the rest of the Spencers."

"Sticks?" She giggled. "You think there's some doubt what we just did validated our mating?"

He shrugged, fighting a smile she could see lifting on the corners of his mouth. "You can never be too careful. We should definitely make sure we have all the bases covered just to be certain."

She flushed, unable to control the heat rising in her skin at the mention of mating again. "I think we might have missed a few bases, in fact. Like second and third. If we crossed home plate, is it considered valid without touching all three other bases?"

He tapped his lips with two fingers. "I don't know, but I'm not taking any chances." Releasing her bicep, he danced his fingers back over her breast. "I'll go back to second base and slow down," he mumbled as he leaned down to kiss her nipple.

Heather sucked in a breath the second his lips hit her skin, feeling the pucker of her nipple and the tightening of her breast.

Marcus's tongue reached out to lick the tip, making her flinch. He cupped the globe firmly with one hand and blew on the nipple, sending a cool breeze that made her squirm.

"So sensitive," he muttered. "I love how responsive you are." He switched to the other breast, treating it the same.

Before long, Heather writhed beneath him as though she hadn't just come twice minutes ago. She couldn't believe how scrambled her brain could become from nothing more than nipple play. She'd never experienced anything like that before. Of course, she'd never been with her mate before, either.

What they said about mating was all true. It was intense and amazing and all-consuming.

Marcus nudged her legs apart with his knee. When his thigh pressed against her center, she moaned. "Marcus." She gripped his arm with her hand as he used his leg to tease her back to full arousal. "Oh, God. What are you doing to me?"

A deep chuckle vibrated through him, humming into her body. "Claiming you."

She squeezed his bicep tighter, her nails digging in so hard she'd surely leave indentations.

Marcus didn't seem to notice. His thigh continued to rub her, lifting and lowering enough to raise the hood of her clit with each pass, exposing the nerve endings to his pressure.

Suddenly his thigh disappeared, and he thrust two fingers into her pussy.

Heather pursed her lips to keep from screaming.

"So wet for me, baby."

She didn't acknowledge his chatter. It had been easier when he'd been silent. His words drove her ardor higher.

And then his lips were on hers, consuming her while he removed his fingers from inside her and lightly stroked her lower lips.

She dueled with his tongue, learning his taste mixed with the mint of her toothpaste.

The slight growth on his chin and face rubbed against hers as he sucked her bottom lip into his mouth and stroked it with his tongue. When he popped free, he looked her in the eye. "I'm one lucky bastard. How did I get so lucky?"

"You?" She shoved him off her and pushed until he landed on his back. If she didn't dislodge his fingers from her pussy, she was going to come again too soon. "So far, all the lucky has been on me."

He smiled up at her. "You're the one who said she was mated to a mutt," he teased.

Heather let her gaze run up and down his body. She hadn't had the opportunity to explore him sufficiently yet. Before he could react and regain control, she threw one leg over him and straddled his thighs. Her hands landed on his chest as he grabbed her forearms.

"Hardly a mutt now..." she whispered. His chest was

broad and firm. He worked out. A lot. A light scattering of hair enticed her. His skin was dark against her pale complexion. His pecs freaking rock solid. "What on earth do you do all day?"

"I work in construction."

"Ahh. That explains it." She lifted her gaze to meet his. Dark brown eyes, the same color she'd watched in his wolf form, stared up at her. His hair was almost black, disheveled, and sexy as hell the way it fell across his forehead.

His full lips were parted, and she could hear each breath he took.

Wiggling free of his hands, she sat up straighter and grazed her fingertips down his torso until she met his cock—thick and hard, jerking to attention as she caressed one finger up its length.

Marcus was as aroused as she was, even after claiming her so recently. The tip of his mushroom-shaped head glistened with precome. Wanting to know his taste, all of him, Heather gathered the semen on her finger and brought it to her mouth.

She met his gaze when he moaned. "Mmm."

"Baby…" He reached for her, his hands cupping her breasts. The gentle touch brought her more fully to life, as if that were possible.

Moisture pooled between her legs, spread wider than ever to encompass his thighs. She leaned forward into his palms, her clit brushing against his cock.

Marcus pinched her nipples between his fingers enough to draw a whimper from her. Her vision blurred, needing him inside her again.

When he released her breasts, he grazed his palms down her belly until he reached her hips, grasping her waist. His hands were large enough that he encompassed her clit with his thumbs, making her lift off him.

"Scoot forward, baby. Lower yourself over me."

She inched closer to his chest on her knees until his cock lodged at her entrance. Holding her breath, she settled her palms on his chest and eased onto his girth.

The stretch was amazing, even though it hadn't been long since he'd last been inside her. In slow motion she settled over him until he was as deep as possible, the filling sensation making her grip at his length with the walls of her sex.

"Lord, that's sexy, Heather. You're going to be the death of me."

She tried to smile, but her mouth wouldn't obey any commands. Instead she spread her fingers over his pecs for leverage, and lifted up, only to impale herself once again over him on a low moan.

Sex with Marcus was unlike anything she'd ever experienced in her life. So much more sensation. Was it because he was so mysterious and sexy? Or was it truly the mating?

Her clit landed on his torso with every pass. She gritted her teeth, not wanting to come too soon. She wanted to enjoy the sensation of having him fill her longer.

Marcus must have read her mind. He stilled her over him, filling her to the hilt. "Don't come yet, baby. Wait for it."

She met his gaze, wondering how on earth she could comply with his words. Staring into his eyes didn't help matters at all. Lust filled his look, his eyes soft, his face full of emotion, his brow furrowed in concentration, his lips parted.

Heather leaned over him and met his lips with hers, melting into his chest as they joined. Her nipples pebbled harder as they brushed his. And Marcus held her hips firmly, not letting her lift off him. He didn't want to come yet, either. The slower pace of this second phase of their mating was delicious.

She waited several heartbeats and then couldn't stand it any longer. When she attempted to lift up and resume the glorious friction, Marcus gripped her harder.

One second she was battling the clutch of his fingers and then next she was flat on her back, her breath whooshing out of her with an *oomph*.

Marcus managed to keep himself buried in her warmth the entire time, and he now hovered over her. "Grab the headboard with your hands, baby. Hold yourself steady."

She lifted her shaky arms over her head and grappled for the rungs. The second she wrapped her palms around the spindles, Marcus pulled her knees up wide and high and removed his cock, only to thrust back into her, pounding with the same intensity she craved. Every time he hit her clit, she nearly came. She turned her face to one side to gasp for oxygen, but her arousal built to a crescendo so fast she couldn't stop it.

In less than a minute, she was at the cusp of the mountain. "Marcus…"

"Come, baby. Come with me."

She shattered, her entire body flinching with each pulse of her pussy around his cock.

Marcus held steady deep inside her, the pulsing of his own orgasm dragging more from her body than she'd thought possible.

When she could finally focus again, she met his gaze, his deep brown eyes penetrating into her soul. "You're amazing. I'm the luckiest mutt on earth."

CHAPTER 5

Marcus watched his mate rest. He'd done so several times. And he'd never tire of watching her face relaxed and at peace. He doubted she was ever as relaxed awake.

When the sun dipped in the sky, he knew they needed to rejoin the family. He had a lot to learn, and his resolve to return home and put an end to his grandfather's plan had not diminished with his mating.

Marcus kissed his mate's forehead and then trailed his lips down her cheek toward her neck. When he stopped to nibble behind her ear, she roused. "You're insatiable," she mumbled.

He grinned. "Only with you. But right now we need to get up."

She groaned and turned toward him, her eyes blinking open. "Now?"

"Yes." He could hear voices coming from the rest of the house. "They're probably getting ready to sit down to dinner. It sure smells like it." He tipped his head back. "Roast, I'm betting."

"That sounds so good. I'm starving."

"Well, get a move on, woman." Marcus hauled her to sitting and then stood to take her arms and lure her farther. "I need to meet with the Spencers and formulate a plan."

"I don't like your so-called plan. It's too dangerous. Too risky." She wrapped her arms around him. "I just got you."

"I know. But there's no better way."

She lifted her gaze to meet his, her chin resting on his chest. "Someone else can do it." She brightened a bit. "You can tell someone all the details, and they can infiltrate the Romulus. Someone from NAR."

He shook his head. "I'm the one who has to go behind the scenes." He rubbed his hands up and down her biceps, trying to soothe her. "I feel a sense of obligation even."

She released him to sit up straighter. "Obligation? Is that what this is about? You think you have to put your life at risk simply because you're related to these people?" She gripped his forearms now. "Please, Marcus. Listen to yourself. That's a horrible reason to go behind the scenes. You could be killed."

He smiled wanly. "That's not the only reason. I'm the only person guaranteed to breach their front line of defense. Think about it. I'm Melvin's grandson. He has no other. He's salivating at the mouth to bring me in. It's not like some random stranger could gain a similar pass. It would take too long, even if they could. I can get inside their facility in a flash." He snapped his fingers to emphasize how important this was.

"I don't like it."

"I know, baby. And if there were any other way, I would jump on it." He understood her pain. They were newly mated. The idea of leaving her anywhere was almost more than he could bear. But he also knew deep in his gut this plan was unavoidable.

"Let's not be hasty. Maybe someone can come up with a better plan."

"We can discuss it for days and never come up with an option that's as viable as this one. You know that."

She looked down at her body. After a pause, she changed the subject. "I need a shower before dinner."

"Take a quick one." He kissed her lips gently, hoping to console her, as well as himself.

"Will you join me?" She lifted her gaze.

"As enticing as that sounds, we don't have time. And I took a shower while you slept."

Heather's shoulders slumped as she trudged from the room. At the door, she paused and turned around. Her gaze was lowered. "We didn't use any condoms. You would know if…" Her voice trailed off.

"You're safe, baby. You aren't ovulating. Yes, I would know."

Her shoulders lowered as tension left her body. She turned, entered the bathroom, and flipped on the shower. She didn't bother closing the door. He liked that.

And she was fast. Impressively so. She reemerged minutes later, toweling her hair dry, her glorious body naked, drips of water clinging to her skin. Her breasts stood high and firm, and her nipples pebbled in the cooler air of the bedroom.

He'd dressed while she showered, and now he stood rooted to his spot watching her as though she were a work of art.

Marcus thought about her last statement before she'd entered the bathroom. It was true he hadn't used a condom. And he hoped he never had to. Just staring at her naked body made him long to see her round with his child. Since when did he visualize anything like that? After the childhood he'd suffered, he'd never considered bringing a child into this world. But now that he'd met Heather, his opinion had changed. He wouldn't impregnate her without her consent, but the idea no longer brought forth the same emotions as it had two days ago.

He watched her while she opened drawers and pulled out panties, a bra, another tank top, and shorts. He would never tire of watching her move around. Even the sway of her hips made him lick his lips. It would be a long time before he had enough of her to sate his appetite.

"If you don't put something on fast, we're going to be right back where we started."

She turned toward him. "And this would be a bad thing?"

He narrowed his gaze, but he smirked at the same time. "Don't tempt me."

Finally, she buttoned her shorts and smiled at him. "Ready."

Marcus opened the door and took her hand. He held her close to his side as they entered the great room.

The family was gathering. Natalie saw them first. "Oh, good. You're here. I was thinking you two might starve in there." She smiled huge as she winked at them. "Dinner's ready."

Marcus returned her warm smile. "I'm starved. Thank you so much again." He glanced around. Drake and his mate weren't there. And for that small concession, Marcus was relieved. He could face that problem later.

"Please. Sit. Let's eat. We can talk again after our stomachs are full." Natalie nodded toward the table as she returned to the kitchen.

Everyone took a seat quickly. An immense amount of food was piled on the table. Indeed there was a roast with all the vegetables, but there were other side dishes scattered around the table also.

"I'm so grateful for your hospitality," Marcus said as he scooted his chair in. "To be honest, it's been a while since I've eaten."

"I figured." Natalie smiled at him as she took her own seat.

Heather set her hand on Marcus's thigh under the table and squeezed.

He nearly spilled the glass of water he'd picked up. He set the drink down, reached under the table, and squeezed her fingers. The imp.

Heather giggled, not so subtly.

No one commented. Of course they all knew newly mated couples were prone to unusual antics. Marcus wouldn't have believed he'd be in such a position someday, lured by the wiles of a sexy woman, but here he was. And her hand on his thigh hardened his cock with a force that punched him in the gut. Everything they said about mating was true. His ardor didn't lessen after claiming his mate. If anything, it was stronger. How was he ever going to leave her?

Marcus piled his plate with several dishes of the best food he'd ever seen. His own mother never cooked a meal like this even for Thanksgiving. Natalie was clearly a fantastic cook.

They ate mostly in silence. Marcus was glad for the reprieve. He really was starving. When he was finished, he felt much better, and he turned to find Heather watching him with a smile on her face.

He lifted a brow.

"Need more?"

"I think I'm good." He kissed her briefly on the lips, unable to resist.

CHAPTER 6

Heather awoke the following morning to the smell of coffee. The sun was high in the sky. She'd slept late. She was burrowed under the covers, but she knew immediately she was alone. The scent of her mate was faint.

Voices from the rest of the house told her he was undoubtedly already working hard with the Spencers to formulate a plan against the Romulus.

Heather took a deep breath and rolled out of bed. Her ankle hit the floor and gave very little protest. *Good. At least I don't have to hobble around all day.*

When she entered the bathroom, she stared at herself in the mirror for a few moments in horror. She looked tired and…well fucked. Embarrassment jerked her awake, and she flipped on the shower immediately, glancing down at her body, her skin covered with a pink flush.

As soon as the water heated, she stepped into the

steam and closed her eyes, luxuriating in the cascade of water. When she finally inhaled slowly and reached for the soap, she took her time.

After the shower, she felt somewhat alive and headed out to find her mate. Her body still tingled at the idea of getting close to him. Even if he was preoccupied all day, at least she would be near.

When she entered the great room, she found Jerome and Scott standing at the table, maps and documents spread out in front of them.

Jerome nodded. "Hey, Heather. Marcus went into town with Drake to get some things. The poor guy has nothing of his own." He glanced at his watch. "I'm sure they'll be back soon."

She crossed to the kitchen counter at the lure of coffee, deflated that her mate was not in the house or even on the property. She blew out a breath. "I'm sure. Nothing like traveling halfway across the country without a single item, including clothes." Her hands shook as she tipped the coffee pot to fill her mug.

Her heart beat faster as she turned back toward the table. "You guys don't waste any time, do you?"

"We can't. We need to act fast." Jerome took a seat in front of a huge map of Minnesota. "Lives are at stake. Marcus feels guilty for waiting as long as he did to come forward. Not that he should, mind you. But he does. And he wants to put an end to whatever his grandfather is up to as much as anyone. I urged him to take a few days, but he's adamant."

"What have you done so far?" Heather asked,

glancing at the array of papers, unease creeping up her spine.

Jerome pointed to the stacks of files. "We filled Marcus in on all the details of the last two months. Evan, the private investigator who spearheaded all this, is coming from St. Louis. And Ralph Jerard, the head elder, is coming from Seattle. He'll have his right-hand man with him, Alex Marshall. We will all meet to discuss the next steps."

"And you're certain it has to be Marcus who infiltrates the Romulus?"

Jerome nodded. "As much as I wish there was another way, this seems like the best option. Melvin Cunningham has no other grandchildren, so he's obviously intent on using his only heir to secure his family line, and not in a good way."

Heather swallowed the bad taste this arrangement gave her. The only thing she could picture was the enormous risk involved in sending the mate she finally joined with yesterday to fake his way behind the scenes of the enemy.

A chill raced down her spine as she sipped her coffee.

Natalie came in through the back door. She smiled and hugged Heather. "I didn't get a chance to properly congratulate you yesterday." She held Heather at arm's length and looked her in the eye. "Happy?"

"Worried is more like it."

Natalie pursed her lips for a second. "Understandable." She turned toward the oven and pulled out a plate. "I saved you some breakfast from the savages. Eat. You'll feel better after a meal."

"Bless you." Heather took the plate and followed Natalie outside to the back porch. When the door shut behind them, blocking out the men's voices and the ominous papers, she felt instant relief. "I can't fathom what this all means."

"I'm sure. Last month, when all of you arrived and my son Daniel realized Allison was his mate, I thought they would both have a coronary sorting through the mess of his involvement with NAR and her precarious safety issues. But they survived, and you will too. It's a bump in the road. When this is all over, you can relax with your mate and live happily ever after."

Heather lifted her gaze. "Do you believe that? I mean that good will prevail in this case? What if the Romulus wins, and we all end up living in a new world?" She shivered. "We may not even be a secret from the general human population by the time this fight is over."

"It's a possibility. But we can only hope it doesn't happen. Now that we know more about who's behind everything, we have the upper hand again. Thanks to Marcus."

"Is it selfish of me to wish he'd never come here?"

Natalie smiled warmly. "Not at all. It's normal. But then you wouldn't have met him, and we wouldn't be sitting here now."

"I could be dead." Heather looked out toward the field where she'd collapsed when the diamondback had bitten her. Had it been just two days ago?

Natalie set a hand on Heather's leg. "But you aren't."

Just as Heather finished eating, having no idea what she'd consumed or how it tasted over the lump in her throat, a truck pulled up and Drake and Marcus headed toward the porch. Marcus's face lit with a smile when he saw her. "Hey, sleepy. I tried to hurry. Have you been up long?" He stepped onto the porch and immediately leaned down to kiss Heather, straddling her with his palms on the arms of her chair.

He had nothing in his hands. She wondered what he'd bought in town and where it was.

"Let's go for a walk."

Natalie took Heather's plate and silently went inside.

Marcus reached for her hand. "It's so nice out this morning before the heat of the day moves in. Come on. I'll watch out for snakes." He grinned at her.

Heather took his hand and let him lead her down the steps and away from the house. They walked in silence for several minutes. Marcus didn't falter in his steps. This wasn't a leisurely stroll. He had a destination in mind.

Her heart beat faster as she kept up with his longer stride. Just being next to him made her pulse beat faster. She held him tight, trying to close the distance between them.

"It's beautiful here." He lifted his gaze to the sky. "I can see why you stayed."

"Yeah. I love it, and the Spencers are wonderful people. They took me in and treat me like their own. I could never repay them."

"And they don't expect you to." He pulled her closer, tucking her under his arm. She warmed. Marcus led her to the edge of the corral and leaned against the fence.

"I spoke to Kenzie earlier."

Heather lifted her gaze to his. "Oh. How'd it go?"

"You were right. She's very gracious. Drake had prepared her. I'm not sure I could be as forgiving if someone treated me the way I treated her at The Gathering."

"Kenzie's very sweet. I expected nothing less." She watched his face, seeing the calm descend. Speaking to Kenzie seemed to have lifted a weight off his shoulders he'd carried a long time.

Marcus cleared his throat. "I want you to tell me what happened to you. All of it. It's niggling at the back of my mind." He paused. "I get the gist of it, but you're my mate and I don't want this unspoken horror between us while we're starting off together."

Heather swallowed. She'd relived her week of terror several times for counselors and The Head Council, and even in group sessions with the other women. They all had a story to tell. And Marcus was right. It would be weird for her not to share what happened with him. Clear the air.

She ducked her head. "I was out jogging near my home in Oregon. It's a small town. I told you that much. Nothing happens there. No real crime. It's the safest place on earth. Or it was." She shivered. It was half the reason she couldn't go back, if she were honest. She'd never feel safe there again.

Marcus tipped her face up. "Go on."

"Someone grabbed me from the road I was jogging on, threw a hood over my head, and tossed me in the trunk of a car so fast, I didn't have time to react." Her voice rose, and she wrung her hands together as she thought back again. It only got marginally easier with each telling. "I fought hard. I swear. But there were several of them, and I'm small. I wasn't strong enough. It was pitch dark under the hood, and they easily wrestled me into the trunk. I tried to kick. I screamed. But no one was around to hear me. A needle jabbed my thigh, and in seconds everything went black.

"When I woke up, I had no idea how long I'd been out or where I was. Someone was carrying my body over their shoulder. I still wore the hood. I didn't know if it was day or night. My arms were tied behind my back, and my feet were strapped together.

"Panic like you can't imagine filled me. My heart raced through the fog of the drugs. I couldn't have escaped even if I hadn't been bound. I was weak, barely lucid.

"Whoever carried me made no attempt to be gentle, which scared the fuck out of me. I thought I was dead for sure. I screamed inside the hood as soon as I could get my voice to work, but all I got in response was laughter.

"The next thing I knew, the man had entered a building. I heard the door shut behind us. His footsteps made more sound on the wood floor. I could smell coffee and cigarette smoke. He took me down some stairs, slamming my body into the sides of the narrow stairwell without a care. When he reached the bottom, he flopped me on a mattress on the floor and injected me again."

Heather looked into Marcus's eyes. They glistened, but he didn't interrupt. His lips were pursed tight. He uncrossed his legs and fisted his hands at his sides. His chest rose and fell.

Heather set her hands on his pecs. "Don't freak. That's about all there is to tell. I spent the next week in that basement. I don't think the men who brought me there were around very much. They didn't stay there. They left me alone most of the time. I had a bathroom, and they left me food and water.

"The worst part was the injections. Scared the fuck out of me. But everything has left my system by now." She wrapped her arms around his middle and held him.

He seemed to need the comfort more than her. It took him several moments to unclench his fists and grasp her, but when he did, it was with tremendous force. He knocked the wind out of her, holding her so tight and burying his face in her hair. "I'm so sorry, baby."

She squirmed to lift her gaze again. "And I'm okay now. I had it better than most. I had enough to eat, and I was only there a week before NAR busted into the house and found me. The other women have much worse tales to tell."

"I don't think I could stand that." Rage lurked beneath the surface. She could see it in his eyes. "If I ever get my hands on those bastards…"

"Well, you probably won't, so don't get your hopes

up. I couldn't describe them if I had to. I only had a few glimpses. They didn't let me see them."

He met her gaze, his eyes hard. "I will find them."

"Marcus…" She didn't know how to finish her thought. The last thing she wanted was for him to go on a rampage traipsing around the country looking for two assholes so he could extract revenge.

He tucked her under his chin and held her against his chest again. "Don't think about it now."

"Okay." As if that were possible. *Sure*. Now she had to worry about him going behind the scenes of the enemy *and* hunting down the assholes who'd kidnapped her.

They stood there for a long time, listening to the horses in the barn and the birds chirping in the trees. Finally Marcus pulled back. "Come on." He took her hand again and led her away with purpose.

"Where're we going?"

"You'll see."

He aimed for the row of cabins on the other side of the corral. She'd stayed in one of the ten cabins when she'd first arrived. Normally they were used for families on dream vacations. The Spencers ran a dude ranch. And one week a month they catered to children with disabilities.

But not for the last few weeks. They'd donated their ranch to help the women and hadn't reopened for regular customers yet. And they wouldn't until they were sure it was safe. It hadn't been long since a massive battle of wolf shifters had been fought right in the middle of the clearing. Humans would have had a heart attack to have seen that. Hell, even regular shifters had a few years shaved off their lives when they saw the size of those enhanced wolves.

Marcus stopped in front of the first cabin and turned to her. He held up a key with a huge grin.

A slow smile spread across Heather's face. "Ah. Splendid idea. Why didn't I think of that?"

"Can't take the credit, actually. Jerome handed me the key this morning with a smirk. We're taking up residence here as of now. Unless it makes you nervous not being in the main house."

She shook her head and pulled up on her tiptoes to kiss his lips. "Not now that you're with me."

"This way no one will hear you when I make you scream my name, except maybe the horses. The barn is closer than the main house. But I spoke with them each earlier, and they promised to keep our secrets." He waggled his eyebrows and turned toward the cabin, pulling her along.

"You spoke with the horses?"

"Uh-huh."

"Just checking. That's what I thought you said."

"You heard me."

She giggled. "And what makes you think you can make me scream your name?"

Marcus opened the cabin door as she spoke. He turned toward her, grabbed her around the waist, and threw her over his shoulder. "Challenge accepted."

Heather squealed and then laughed. "You're on."

"Baby, you don't know who you're messing with. By the end of the day, I'll have you begging for mercy."

"Really?" She held on to his shirt as he entered the cabin, kicked the door shut, and strode straight to the small bedroom. Plastic shopping bags littered the floor. Ah, so he'd stopped here and dropped off his purchases before finding her.

He tossed her into the center of the bed and raised an eyebrow.

She stared up at him, unable to breath. Goose bumps rose on her skin as his gaze narrowed with lust.

Heather reached for the hem of her shirt and lifted it over her head. She unbuttoned her shorts, slowly lowered the zipper, and then lifted her hips provocatively to wiggle them over her thighs. "Are you just going to stand there?"

Marcus hadn't moved. In fact, he leaned against the dresser, watching her. His face had lost the mirth of a minute ago. His gaze strayed up and down her body, now clad in only her matching bra and panty set. "Enjoying the show. Keep going."

Heather inhaled long and slow as her body betrayed her, her pussy tightening at his tone of voice. She bit her lower lip and squirmed out of her panties and then popped off her bra. She piled everything on the end of the bed.

Marcus stared at her until she shivered. "God, you're sexy." He righted himself from the dresser and sauntered toward her. "I don't know what I did to deserve this."

"I could say the same thing."

"It's only been a little over a year since I attempted to mate not one but two unwilling women in one evening against their will. I was an ass. I deserved a longer celibacy sentence."

Heather inhaled sharply. "That wasn't your fault."

He shook his head. "I know that, intellectually, but it doesn't change what I did. It doesn't change how I made those women feel. And it doesn't change the guilt I have for the way I treated them."

"It's only been one month since I was abducted and held against my will for an entire week. I understand your guilt. Do you think I don't question my part in that every single day?"

"What part did you have in it? There's nothing you could have done."

"Really? What if I'd fought harder? Chosen a different route that day to run? Maybe I didn't scream loud enough. Maybe I was dressed too provocatively."

Marcus leaned over the bed, grasped her shins, and pulled her closer until she fell onto her back, straddling him near the edge of the bed. "That's ridiculous, baby. You couldn't control any of those things."

"Yeah? And your guilt isn't just as ridiculous after a man you should have been able to trust drugged you with enough stupid sex serum to make you irrational?"

He stared down at the *V* of her legs, his fingers inching up her thighs toward her center. Finally he lifted his gaze and spoke again. "So we're both in the same boat. Maybe we can work through these issues together?"

"I'd like nothing more. Now, take off some clothes so I don't start feeling self-conscious."

He gave her a small smile as he released her to kick

off his shoes and tug off the rest of his clothes to drop them haphazardly on the floor.

Her skin prickled with goose bumps. It was warm in the cabin. She could hear the whir of the air conditioner, so he must have come earlier and turned it on, but it hadn't cooled down enough to chill her skin. The goose bumps were from nerves.

CHAPTER 7

His dick nearly ached from wanting her. It bobbed against him, pulsing prematurely.

Heather scooted back across the bed as he approached and crawled up next to her. When he reached her side, her face dipped as she gazed at the length of his body. "Lie back," she insisted. "I need some time to explore. I've barely seen you naked."

Marcus flopped onto his back, his cock stiffening further at the way she took him in with her gaze.

She leaned over him, shocking him, her eyes glued to his length, her mouth open. Without pausing, she reached with one hand and delicately stroked a finger up the top of his cock until it flicked over the head.

So much for exploring. That act was zero to sixty in less than a second. He'd never last through her perusal.

Marcus cupped her breast with one hand, letting his thumb flick over her nipple, hoping to distract her enough to slow down her process and possibly save him some embarrassment. He gritted his teeth against the need to come. She deserved this concession. However, if anyone could make him come with her gaze alone, it would be Heather.

Marcus continued to graze his fingers over her breast while she wrapped her hand around his girth and gently pumped up and down the length. He squeezed his eyes closed to concentrate on the feel of her wrapped around him.

When her tongue flicked the head, his eyes jerked wide. He hadn't realized she'd leaned so far forward. He gripped her breast and pinched his lips together.

Suddenly Heather sucked his length deep into her mouth.

Holy mother of God.

Her cheeks hollowed as she firmly established her authority over his cock. He would forever be putty in her hands if she was going to do this very often. And he was powerless to stop her.

The little imp had a wicked mouth that threatened to drain his balls before he reached the back of her throat. And God how he wanted her to suck him farther.

She moaned and took him deeper.

Tiny noises coming from Heather vibrated against his cock, making him stiffen more. He lifted his torso to meet her thrusts. Even though he still held her nipple between his fingers, he couldn't concentrate on anything but his growing need. He gripped the sheets with his other hand, attempting to judge the moment he would need to pull out. He didn't want to force her to swallow him.

In one powerful second, Heather slipped lower, her face almost touching his pelvis. She tightened her grip with her lips, and Marcus could hold back no longer. He came, deep in her throat, his cock pulsing so hard one would think he'd never had an orgasm before.

He released her nipple and lifted his hand to thread his fingers into her hair.

She never hesitated. Her free hand toyed with his balls, weighing them and learning their texture. When had she begun to fondle him there?

When he finally relaxed, easing the tension from his tight ass and thighs, he groaned. He was doomed to this mate of his. His life would never be the same. Sated, he managed to pull her off his cock and settle her against his side with her head on his chest. He kissed the top of her head and stroked her hair. Glorious red locks lay spread all across both of them.

But he needed more. It wasn't enough that he just came. Somehow the act didn't sate him. He wanted to hear her scream, as he'd threatened on the front porch.

With the hand wrapped around her middle, he held her tight. He lifted his knee to force her legs open, his thigh pressing against her pussy.

Heather sucked in a breath and wiggled against him, her wetness dripping onto his leg.

He grabbed her thigh with his free hand and pulled it higher, opening her wider. And then he reached across her ass and stroked his fingers down her crack until he could stroke through her folds.

She moaned, squirming against him, her hands

pressing against his chest in an attempt to dislodge herself from his grip.

He held tighter to her waist. "Where do you think you're going?" he teased.

She inhaled sharply as he finished his question by thrusting two fingers inside her. Her hips bucked toward him this time as she gave up the fight. Or forgot to keep it up.

"I love your little sounds, baby. But I want to hear more."

She groaned as her head rolled back and forth against his chest.

Marcus smiled. He was making headway. He pulled her moisture from inside her pussy to drag it around her clit until she held her breath.

"What's the matter, baby?"

"God, Marcus. I need you. Please…" A long breath escaped her lips against his chest.

"You need what, exactly?"

"I need you inside me," she whispered. "Please."

He added a finger and thrust three into her fast and deep. "Like that?"

She whimpered. "No. Please, Marcus. Let me climb on top of you." She made a lame attempt to press against him, undoubtedly knowing full well he was way too strong for her.

He dragged his fingers across her G-spot, his grip on her waist keeping her firmly in place.

Short gasps from her mouth told him he'd hit the mark. Her moisture increased, and he withdrew his fingers to circle her clit again, not quite making contact with the little nub.

Heather lifted her hips the tiny fraction available to her, trying to cause his fingers to do what she wanted.

"You challenged me," he reminded her. "I'm just making good on that."

She lifted her face enough to meet his gaze. Her eyes were wide. "I hate to disappoint you, but I'm not a screamer."

Marcus could feel the grin spreading wider across his face until his cheeks ached. "You did not just say that."

She turned a deep shade of red and pushed on his chest. "It's true."

"Correction. It *was* true."

She froze.

"And then you met me." If they had to stay in this bed all day and all night, he would make his woman scream. He had no doubt. To emphasize his position, he thrust his fingers into her again, dragging them out faster and harder, knowing his thumb pressed against her clit with each pass.

Her eyes drooped as she went cerebral on him. Good. She probably had no idea her fingernails dug into his pecs.

When she gasped, he let up. He didn't want her to come until he was sure she could do it without holding back her sound. He needed her so aroused she couldn't keep from screaming.

She panted as he slowed his movements and avoided her clit.

"So wet for me, baby." He kissed her damp forehead and then let his lips linger on her skin. "Does that feel good?" he asked against her.

"Mmm. Why did you stop? I was so close." Her voice was barely above a whisper.

"Mmm," he mimicked. "I'm not interested in making you come, baby."

She sucked in a breath.

That wasn't entirely true. He had every intention of bringing her to orgasm, but he intended for it to happen around a great deal of involuntary noise. He stroked her lower lips, drawing out more of her moisture and dragging it up toward her tight hole.

She breathed heavily as he approached, her ass cheeks squeezing together, but she didn't protest physically or verbally, so he continued to experiment, circling the puckered entrance and then pressing one finger against it. She stiffened, and he eased off. Later…

Caressing back down to her pussy, he spread her lips apart and then entered her again with short jabs.

Heather immediately shot back into a more aroused state, her body squirming futilely in his grip.

He didn't give her an inch of leeway. Instead he thrust three fingers into her without warning and braced for her to attempt escape. He nudged her knee higher against his abdomen and held it with his forearm, wishing he had one or two spare arms.

"Marcus…" Her voice was just shy of begging.

"Wanna hear that louder, baby."

"I'm so horny. Please, let me come."

"I will. When I'm ready."

The frustration in the strange sound she emitted made him smile.

Marcus pressed two fingers into her, stroked them over her G-spot, and went to work on her clit with his thumb.

She jerked in his grip, struggling against him.

He flicked her clit faster, applying more pressure, realizing the key to the intensity of her arousal lay in the nerve endings beneath her little nub.

Heather moaned. Her head rolled to one side as she gave up the fight against him and enjoyed the sensations.

He wanted to whisper sweet words to her about letting go and succumbing to his touch, but he feared he would interrupt the build inside her with his voice.

Instead, he continued the slow torture that would lead to an intense orgasm. He could tell by her body language she was no longer trying to struggle against him. Her hips pressed toward him instead of bucking away. Her legs spread wider of their own accord. She wanted what he gave…and more.

Finally, she sucked in a deep breath, completely unaware of the continuous moan escaping her lips.

Marcus hoped he judged her correctly as he used his pointer and thumb to pinch her clit hard.

Heather screamed. Her orgasm rushed to the surface so fast, it shocked even him. Her pussy pulsed around his fingers while her clit throbbed between his pinch.

It took several moments for her noises to subside to whimpers and her body to begin to squirm against his thigh in effort to dislodge his touch.

Marcus slowed down gradually until he barely stroked her. "That was so fucking sexy," he mumbled against her forehead.

She groaned. "I can't believe you did that. I've never…"

"I know, baby, and I'm so glad I was your first. It wasn't my name this time, but your scream was still music to my ears. I'll cut you some slack for forgetting my name at that particular moment." He chuckled against her.

Heather swatted his chest with her palm.

He lifted her chin to see her eyes. "I know it's soon, but I'm falling in love with you. It's not just the mating."

She smiled at him. "Too late. I was already in love with you the moment you nudged me with your wet snout in that field. The look in those brown eyes took my breath away. I may have been dazed from the snake bite, but the concern and total fear in your gaze melted my heart."

He wrapped her in both arms and held her tight. How was he ever going to leave her here to infiltrate the Romulus?

∽

A light rap at the front door dragged Marcus from sleep. He tipped his head to find his mate snuggled against him, a peaceful expression on her face.

The knocking sounded again. He had to get up.

As he eased himself out from under his mate, he groaned. He reached for his jeans, pulled them on, and tugged on the zipper. He didn't bother to button the top.

In only a few strides he was at the front door, opening it to find Drake on the porch. "Sorry, man."

Marcus nodded, running a hand through his hair. As much as he hated to admit it, there were far more important things happening than his need to fuck like a rabbit.

"Ralph Jerard, Alex Marshall, and Evan Harmon will be here in an hour. Dad wanted me to come tell you."

Marcus nodded. "I'll be there."

Drake stepped away quickly, a smirk on his face. It was no secret newly mated couples couldn't resist each other, and Drake could not have forgotten that detail in the year since he'd met his mate.

With a soft snick, Marcus shut the door and returned to his mate. He found her pulling herself to sitting. "Why does sex make me so tired? What time is it?"

Marcus glanced at the clock. "One." He was starving, and she had to be also. He couldn't resist approaching her, though. He pulled her to the side of the bed and held her face with both hands to kiss her deeply. He moaned into her mouth. "I wish we had more time."

"I wish you'd abandon this entire idea and stay with me."

He set his forehead against hers. "I know. But we only have an hour right now. We need to head to the main house so I can meet with Jerard and his men."

Heather lowered her hand down his body, dipped

her fingers inside his jeans, and stroked his cock. "An hour is a long time."

"It is." He spread her legs with both hands and nestled between them. "Far more time than we need." He chuckled. At the rate they were going at it, they managed to come every time they got near each other within moments, almost without provocation.

Marcus pulled her closer, until her ass barely balanced on the edge of the mattress. He leaned in until the zipper of his jeans rubbed her pussy, making her moan.

Every time he took her, she loosened up more. Whatever hesitation she had about fully giving herself over to him was dissipating.

He kissed her, holding her face with both hands and melting her with his tongue against her own.

She wrapped her legs around his thighs, pressing her pussy against his jeans.

He needed to be inside her, and he needed more dominance this time. He thought she was ready. Releasing her lips, he eased out of her embrace.

She didn't protest. After all, what more were they going to accomplish with his jeans on?

As soon as he wiggled the denim down his legs and stepped out, he grabbed her waist and flipped her around so fast, she squealed. "What the…?"

He nudged her forward on all fours and climbed up behind her. "I want to take you from behind this time, okay?" He stroked her hair off her neck so he could see her face as she twisted it back to look at him.

She swallowed and nodded, her ass pushing back toward him.

Marcus set one hand on her back and nudged her knees apart with one of his. He stroked her folds with his free hand until she writhed, wiggling so much he couldn't maintain any particular contact. He removed his fingers and pressed on her ass. "Lie down, baby."

She twisted her neck back to look at him again. "Flat?"

"Yep." He gently applied pressure to her lower back. "Lie on your stomach." It was the only way he could think to keep her from squirming so much.

His cock bobbed in front of him as he watched her comply. At the last second, he grabbed a pillow and stuffed it under her belly. For a minute, he simply caressed her skin, up and down her back and across her ass cheeks. "Spread your legs for me, baby."

She inched her knees apart one at a time, and he crawled between her spread legs to keep them open.

With one hand on her lower back once again, he used the other hand to stroke through her folds and dip into her warmth. "Baby, you're so ready for me already." He didn't know why he was surprised. His cock felt close to exploding without any contact.

He couldn't hold back another second, so he lowered himself between her legs and lined his cock up with her entrance. As he pressed into his mate, surrounding himself with her tight sheath, he groaned. He held still for several heartbeats, leaning down to encompass her entire body with his, his chest against her back, his hands moving up her arms until he threaded her fingers with his above their heads.

And then he eased out of her, teeth tightly gritted. No way could he keep this slow. When Heather lifted her torso into his thrust, he sped up his motions, fucking her fast and hard, squeezing her fingers in his grip and nuzzling her neck with his face.

He groaned into the curve of her neck as he reached the edge of sanity. "Come with me, Heather."

She stiffened, her body telling him she was right with him, and he let go, his release coming so fast he couldn't stop it. He continued to thrust into her as she came around his cock, until they were both spent. Without withdrawing, he let the bulk of his weight relax against his mate, knowing he was too heavy for her but loving the way she felt enveloped by his entire frame.

"You're smashing me," she finally muttered into the pillow.

He eased off reluctantly, letting his cock pop from her warmth and dragging his body to her side.

"Oh God," she said again into the pillow. "You're going to be the death of me."

"I hope not. I like having you around." He playfully swatted her ass. "I hate to say this, but we have to shower and get to the main house."

She flinched. "I don't think I can stand, let alone bathe."

Marcus kissed her ass again and tugged her to the edge of the bed. "I'll make you a sandwich while you shower and then trade you places."

She groaned. "I'd rather you joined me."

He smiled. "Me too, baby, but we'd never make it out of this cabin if I did."

~

Thirty minutes later, Heather settled against her mate's side as they walked toward the main house.

Nerves ate a hole in her. Whatever was going to happen in this meeting, she knew she wasn't going to like it. The last thing in the world she wanted was for Marcus to leave and travel halfway across the country to pretend to cater to his grandfather. If anyone got wind of his lie, she knew they would kill him. Kin or not.

They entered through the back door, but voices in the living room told Heather several people were already gathered before they entered the house.

Sure enough, she recognized the leader of The Head Council, Ralph Jerard, easily. The other two men had to be Alex Marshall and Evan Harmon.

Jerard stood. He held out a hand to Marcus and smiled. "So good to meet you. I recognize you now. You look a lot like your father and grandfather."

Marcus took his hand. "On the outside. But I can assure you, sir, I'm nothing like them on the inside."

"Well, that's a relief." He motioned toward the man who stood at his side. "This is my assistant, Alex Marshall."

Marcus shook his hand.

The younger man rose from his seat also. "Evan Harmon."

"Marcus Cunningham. Nice to meet you." They shook hands also, and then Marcus introduced Heather. "This is my mate, Heather. She was one of the women rescued last month in the sting."

Heather shook hands with all three men, and they all took a seat. Jerome, Drake, Natalie, and Scott were also there. Several chairs had been brought in from the kitchen.

Jerard began. "First of all, let me thank you for coming forward with this invaluable information. I knew we had a mole. I just didn't know who it was. No wonder the Romulus was always one step ahead of us. If Melvin was feeding them information almost before we shared it, we didn't stand a chance.

"I've been communicating with Evan for months on a private cell, but fat lot of good it did if Melvin listened in. I knew we had an insider, I just hoped it wasn't one of the other four head elders."

"Have you confronted him, sir?" Marcus asked.

Jerard shook his head vehemently. "No. And I'm not going to. We need to discuss this and come up with a plan. I don't want him getting wind we're on to him. That could become valuable eventually. Tell me everything you know. I got the story from Jerome, but I want to hear it again in your words."

Heather listened intently as Marcus retold the tale of his childhood and everything he'd been through since he'd started taking strange drugs. It didn't get easier listening to it a second time. She ached for him. For the boy mistreated with no champion on his side. She hoped she never had to meet his parents. She couldn't imagine being polite.

Suddenly Marcus slapped his leg. "I've got it." He'd finished his story, and they were brainstorming about what to do next. "I've been wracking my brain trying to figure out how to reinsert myself. I've been gone a month. I couldn't come up with an explanation that sounded feasible."

"What then?" Jerome asked.

Heather held her breath as Marcus responded, "I met my mate."

"So?" Evan leaned forward.

"I can't very well return without telling them that anyway. They would sense it immediately. So, I go back, and my excuse for disappearing without mention is I met my mate. A month ago instead of two days ago."

Jerard scratched his chin. "It could work."

Heather groaned inwardly, realizing her plan to never make the acquaintance of his family just flew out the window. "So we return together."

Marcus flinched and twisted to look at her. "No." He shook his head. "No way. Not willing to put you in the line of danger."

Everyone seemed to hold their breaths.

Heather waited for him to think.

Jerome spoke first. "She's right. Why else would you return home except to show off your new mate?"

Marcus visibly swallowed. He turned his gaze back to the group. "So we come up with another plan. I'm not taking Heather."

Heather's face burned. She wasn't sure if she was

angry with his highhanded command or flattered he cared so much.

She went with pissed. She stood, releasing the grip she had on his arm. "It's not your decision to make. If I'm willing to put myself at risk, you can't stop me."

Marcus jerked his gaze toward her, shock evident in his wide gaze.

Good. He needed to know what it felt like for his mate to walk into the face of danger.

"Heather—"

She shook her head. "No. I'm not kidding. It's a solid plan. I hate it as much as you do. The last thing I want to do is make nice and smile at your misguided parents, but if you insist on going back, I'm going with you. You need a plausible explanation for where you've been. And you'll need to agree to go to that damn facility willingly with your grandfather and gather intel. Unless one of you can come up with a better plan ASAP, I'm in as deep as you."

Silence.

Marcus visibly breathed hard. He swallowed.

No one interrupted.

"What? No better ideas, mutt?" She set her hands on her hips.

Drake chuckled.

Jerard laughed. "That's rich. Love to hear the backstory on that one."

Marcus didn't stop piercing her with his gaze.

Jerome cleared his throat. "Let's discuss this rationally."

Heather didn't think rational was in Marcus's

vocabulary right then. Clearly, what applied to him didn't extend to her.

Marcus held out a hand toward Heather. "Please. Sit back down."

She eased onto the couch next to him, but she didn't take his extended hand.

Jerome continued. "She has a point, Marcus. I know it wasn't what you had in mind when the idea hit you to go back home, but she's right. You need a plausible excuse for your absence, and this is the best one I can think of."

"She was kidnapped by these people," he nearly screamed. "I can't just bring her back to them on a silver platter."

Jerome paused and then continued. "I bet your parents don't know that. They probably don't even know women were kidnapped and then rescued. If they do, they surely don't know Heather was specifically one of them. It's not like your grandfather would be at your parents' home waiting on your return.

"You show up. Introduce all lovey dovey like. Smiles. Excitement. The whole works. It's totally believable. So many wolves meet their mates and drop off the planet for a while. You steer the conversation to what's happening in the world because you've been out of the loop for so long. Your parents take the bait and think they're luring you in. I'm sure Cunningham put the fear of God in them to find you and get you to his facility."

"So then what? I willingly go to this mystery place in Minnesota and then call you guys?"

"Basically, yes."

"And where is Heather during that part? I'm not about to take her there, besides someone might know who she is. Hell, my grandfather might have seen pictures of her. What if she meets him at my parents' house and he recognizes her?" Marcus shook his head. "I don't like this."

"I never met your grandfather personally, so hopefully we're safe on that front. I'll say I need to visit my family in Oregon after the visit and pretend to leave to go see them." She hated the idea, but it was solid.

Alex spoke next. "I'll make sure she's in a safe place, Marcus. The minute you leave, I'll pick her up."

Marcus ducked his head with an audible sigh. He set his elbows on his knees and leaned his forehead on his palms.

Heather set a hand on his back. She rubbed toward his shoulders and leaned over to comfort him with her cheek on his bicep. "I'll be safer than what you're going to do," she whispered. "The entire idea of you infiltrating these bastards makes my stomach revolt."

He turned to look at her and hauled her into his embrace. "Why do you have to be so damn rational?"

She smiled. Finally, he was coming around.

They spent the next two hours outlining their plan. NAR would insert a tracking chip in Marcus before they left the ranch. Heather and Marcus would go to his parents' house like nothing ever happened. They would enter happy as clams, declare their mating, and then help guide his parents to mention Marcus needed to go to the facility in Minnesota. Everyone doubted they understood the complete nature of the facility.

Nevertheless, they would encourage their only child to turn himself over to those bastards.

Heather would leave as though she were heading to Oregon to visit her family. In reality she would meet up with Alex and other members of NAR so they could take her somewhere safe.

A full team from NAR would follow Marcus and his grandfather to Minnesota and prepare to take over the facility.

It sounded foolproof enough.

Why did Heather feel like her life was ending?

CHAPTER 8

Marcus leaned against the door to their cabin the second they entered, pushing it shut with his butt and hauling Heather into his arms. He pulled her head back to meet his gaze with a grip on her curls. "You're shaving years off my life expectancy, you know that?"

She grinned up at him and lifted onto her tiptoes to kiss his lips. Then she shrugged. "Not any worse than what you're doing to me."

"I need you."

"I've needed you again since before we left the cabin." She slipped from his grip, ducking to get out from under his arms, and then she dodged him when he reached for her.

Meeting his gaze, she crossed her arms, gripped the bottom of her shirt, and lifted it slowly over her head. Her breasts were so full, they were barely contained in her bra.

Marcus prowled forward in slow motion, enjoying the show.

Heather jumped back, giggling.

"You tease."

"You overbearing mutt."

Marcus couldn't stop from chuckling. "I deserve that."

"Yes. You do." She continued to back up until her ass hit the refrigerator in the small kitchenette.

"You're out of space." He encroached on her, set his hands on either side of her head, and pressed his denim-covered cock into her belly.

"You're bigger than me. The field isn't even." Her voice had lowered to the point of almost a whisper.

"And don't you forget it." As he leaned forward, intent on capturing her mouth again, she ducked and squirmed out from his hold to dart across the room and disappear into the bedroom.

Marcus shook his head and groaned, but he couldn't deny how hot she made him in her playful state. He adjusted his cock and went after her.

By the time he got to the bedroom, she'd removed her shorts and was lowering her panties over her hips. "Why am I always less dressed than you?" She backed up and lifted herself onto the bed, still facing him.

"Because I like it that way. Helps me control my need to consume you too fast. If I were naked right now, my cock would already be buried in your sweet pussy." He approached her like a predator to his prey. And the way she insisted on teasing him made the thought all the more accurate.

""You're a tease." He strode forward slowly, precisely.

When he reached the bedside, she sucked in a breath. He could imagine what his expression might look like.

Marcus lifted his gaze gradually up her body, loving every curve.

She caught her lower lip between her teeth.

He climbed onto the bed, eased her onto her back, and kneeled between her legs. He set his hands on her thighs and pressed them open. She was already so wet, and her legs shook. "I think I could make you come with my breath."

She whimpered.

"You're so horny right now. It's sexy." He pulled her folds apart with both hands and inhaled deeply of her scent, memorizing it, as if he would ever forget. He couldn't imagine one hour without her, let alone days while he helped The Head Council gather intel.

He shook the thought from his mind. He needed to ground himself in the here and now, enjoy his mate, and satisfy her to the point she wouldn't be able to sleep properly while they were apart. Give her something to dream about.

Marcus leaned down and stroked the flat top of his tongue from her pussy to her clit.

Heather wiggled against him.

He lifted his face to see hers. "I love it when you squirm."

Her chest rose and fell under his gaze, and he couldn't resist reaching out to cup both breasts in his hands, kneading them and flicking his thumbs over the nipples until they were stiff peaks.

Heather's head lolled to one side. Her eyes fluttered shut.

And then he settled back between her legs and stared at her pussy. He didn't touch her for a long time, knowing the anticipation would make her crazy.

His first touch was to tap her clit, making her lurch her ass upward, her only purchase being her ankles digging into the mattress. She wadded up the sheets on both sides of her body and fisted the linen.

Without touching her anywhere else, he continued to tap her clit.

When she hummed out loud, he used his other hand to pull the hood back so he could tap the swollen nub directly.

A tiny yelped escaped Heather's lips.

"Feel good, baby?"

She didn't respond. Her head rolled to the other side.

So sexy… Finally, Marcus couldn't stand it another minute. He needed her as much as he needed his next breath. He dipped two fingers into her pussy, drew out the moisture, and dragged her arousal across her clit, pressing hard. "Come."

Heather arched her neck and stiffened. Her heels dug into the mattress, and she lifted her ass off the sheets against his pressure as she came. He felt the pulse deep in her clit, indicating her orgasm was forceful.

As she came down, he gradually released the hold on her clit until he simply stroked the little nub, circling it and pinching gently.

Heather moaned. She reached for his hands. "It's too much. So sensitive."

"I know, baby. Let it build again. You're so gorgeous like this." He pried her hands off his wrist with his free hand and lowered them back to the mattress one at a time.

He recognized the moment the sensitivity switched to renewed pleasure.

"Oh, God," she murmured. "Please, Marcus. I need you inside me."

He couldn't stand the intense pressure in his cock another moment. He needed to be inside her at least as much. As her mouth opened farther, no more sound coming out, he realized she'd gotten close to a second orgasm.

Marcus straightened to wiggle out of his jeans as fast as possible.

Heather bit her lower lip again. "Oh, God," she repeated. Her voice was deeper. "I can't…"

She didn't need to. He wanted to be inside her when she let go for the second time, feel the way her pussy gripped his cock and let her orgasm wash through her body.

And he wasn't disappointed.

The second he thrust inside her, she screamed his name. "Marcus."

Music to his ears. Marcus pumped into her several times, holding himself over her with his elbows. Finally he lowered himself so his chest brushed against her nipples. She held on by a thread, her mouth open again, no sound coming out.

God he loved her. The feeling was deep and true. And his cock wouldn't wait.

The second she sucked in a breath and held it, he spoke, "Come, Heather. Now."

She tensed, her entire body rigid as she screamed around her orgasm, her pussy grabbing him and sucking his own orgasm from his cock. He held his breath also as he thrust one last time and let his come pulse against her cervix.

Sweat beaded on his back. He could feel it running down into the hollow above his ass. He couldn't bring himself to pull out of her, though. He smiled as he lowered to take her lips.

Her mouth was still open, and it took her a moment to respond. He muttered against her mouth. "What's the matter, baby? You can't control your lips yet?" he teased.

Snapping back to reality, she closed her mouth with a soft sigh. "Mmm."

Marcus nibbled around her lips until she responded. Soon he had her in a deep kiss she returned with so much energy that he almost lost himself in her again. When he pulled back, he stared into her eyes. "That was so beautiful."

Heather wrapped her arms around his head. "You never cease to amaze me."

"In a good way, I hope?" He chuckled. Being inside her was home.

"Always." She pulled his head back with her fingers wrapped in his hair. "Feed me. You make me so hungry."

He reluctantly let himself slip from her pussy and gathered her in his arms. "Food? You want to eat?" he teased. His stomach growled on cue, and he chuckled, the vibrations shaking both of them. "Okay, but how about naked, and the moment we finish eating I enjoy some dessert."

She lifted on one elbow. "You're insatiable."

He smiled. "All right. If you'd rather play Monopoly later, I'm good with that."

She swatted at his chest and lifted to a sitting position. "Feed me first, and then we'll negotiate dessert."

CHAPTER 9

Heather squeezed her mate's hand as they settled into first class seats on the plane the next morning. "I've never flown in first class," she whispered for his ears only.

"Me neither." He winked at her. "Nice of The Head Council to make us comfortable on the way to the slaughter."

She slapped his leg playfully. "Stop it. Don't remind me. I'm stressed enough. I don't need you to make it worse."

"Hey it was your idea to come with me. I was content to leave you safely on the ranch."

"And say what to your parents about where you've been hiding for a month?"

"I'd have thought of something." He threaded his fingers with hers and lifted her hand to kiss the back of it.

"Yeah, well, my story is far more plausible than anything you would have come up with."

"Woman, you're too feisty." His eyes twinkled.

They spoke during the flight about what they would say when they reached his parents' house. They'd been over it a dozen times the night before, but making sure their stories were straight gave Heather more peace of mind.

By the time they landed in Des Moines and had settled in a rental car, she'd memorized every detail about Marcus she would have acquired in a month of time. No one would believe they had known each other for a month if she didn't pick his brain for info and vice versa.

"How far is it to your parents'?"

"About an hour north." He pulled onto the highway and sped up. His grip on the steering wheel told her everything she needed to know. He was stressed. His brow was furrowed, and he lost interest in conversation as he got closer. Meeting with his parents after what he'd overheard the last time he'd been to the house wouldn't have made the short list of things he ever wanted to do again in this lifetime.

And now, not only was he returning, but he was bringing her with him, and he was going to play fake nice in hopes neither parent realized he was full of shit.

Heather didn't think the task would be as difficult as he imagined. After all, even if he acted somewhat strange in their eyes, newly mated men were known to act strange. It would be expected and easily attributed to his new standing.

The hour passed quickly.

"We're almost there," Marcus announced as he

pulled off the highway. "Last chance to bail out." He glanced at her. His smile only lifted on one side. She knew it was a perfect reflection of his meaning. He was only half kidding.

"If you insist on doing this, I'm not hanging behind. We go together or not at all."

He nodded, his lips pursed. They'd argued about this so many times, it was sounding like a broken record. Neither of them was happy about the other's involvement.

Minutes later he pulled into the driveway of a small, older home. His parents had a large property, as expected. Most shifters who lived in communities with humans lived as privately as possible to avoid detection.

As soon as they stepped out of the car, the front door opened and an older woman Heather assumed was Marcus's mother stepped out. Her hand flew to her mouth as soon as she spotted them. She stood so still, Heather thought she might faint.

Marcus rounded the car and took Heather's hand before walking toward his mother. "Mom." He smiled. Heather thought it looked genuine.

In any case, there was no way he would have trouble fooling his mother because the woman already had tears in her eyes. More than likely, all she could see was the return of the prodigal son. "Marcus." Her voice was soft and gentle, and her gaze shifted to Heather as soon as they reached the steps. "Oh." Her hand flew to her heart. Her smile spread wider. "Oh my."

Heather actually felt a pang of sorrow for the

woman. It would have been a touching moment. It should have been. It was...for Lora Cunningham.

They faced off for several seconds just feet away.

Marcus cleared this throat. "Mom, this is Heather. My mate."

She trembled as she lowered her hand from her chest as she looked toward Heather again. "So nice to meet you. I had no idea."

Marcus dipped his face sheepishly, brilliantly. "Yeah." He shuffled a toe against the porch. "I'm sorry. I haven't been able to bring myself to share her yet." His face was pink with embarrassment when he lifted his gaze.

Heather was amazed at his ability to act.

His mother smiled. "Well, you're here now." She motioned with a wave of her hand. "Come. Goodness. Come inside." She opened the door and held it for them to pass. When they were in the front room, she scurried past them. "Sit. I'll get you drinks."

"Mom, you don't have to do that. We're fine. We've eaten."

"Oh. Okay." The woman was flustered. She lowered herself into a chair. She set her palm on her chest. "I was afraid something had happened to you." Tears still trickled, and she wiped them away with the back of her hand.

Marcus led Heather to the couch and pulled her down next to him. Heather found it impossible to believe this sweet woman was involved in anything as sinister as allowing her own father to drug her only child.

"I can't believe you're here. We've been so worried. Your father will be so relieved."

I'll bet he will. Heather smiled. She could only hope it was genuine enough to not raise suspicion.

"I'm sorry, Mom," Marcus repeated. "As soon as I met Heather, I fell into a trance and couldn't seem to come out of it." He squeezed her hand.

"When did you meet? Where? We went by your house so many times. You were never there."

"Yeah. We met about a month ago, right honey?" He cocked his head toward hers in fake confirmation.

Heather rolled her eyes at him. "Twenty-seven days." She play-slapped his arm as though he were a dolt not to have their exact date of mating memorized.

He smile and leaned forward to touch her nose with his.

It was the most awkward ridiculous act Heather could imagine. It wasn't as though they were faking they were mates, but it felt that way. Heather shivered.

"I suck at details, honey. You know I do."

"True." She rolled her eyes again. "He can't keep day and night separated lately. I think he's in deeper than I am." She turned to make sure Lora was buying the interaction.

The woman had a huge grin as though she were reading a romance novel and the hero and heroine were about to fade to black behind closed doors. "That's so sweet."

"I know that's not true, my love. If I remember correctly, someone asked for pancakes at about one in the morning a few weeks ago."

Heather batted her eyes. "I was hungry." She shrugged.

"Anyway, it was a Sunday, right honey?" He continued without waiting for Heather's response. "I had gone for a run in the huge forest area I like to go to west of here. You know the one, right?" He glanced from Heather to his mom.

His mother nodded, her grin pasted.

"Heather was there with friends. She was visiting from Oregon. We were both shifted, of course."

Lora gasped. "You were shifted when you met?"

"Yep. It was weird. And perfect. And don't feel too bad, because I haven't met her parents yet, either. They live in Oregon. We haven't seen more than a few people since we met."

"You came here first." It wasn't really a question, more of an acknowledgement of her priority in his life.

Marcus gave a sheepish grin again and tilted his head. "Well, you were closer. And I felt guilty... eventually. I've been selfish." He wrapped his arm around Heather and squeezed her to his side. "It wasn't hard."

She lifted her face to briefly kiss his lips. "I finally called my parents at least, but they weren't expecting me. I intended to spend the fall with my friends at their place a few hours west of here before I started searching for a job."

"Anyway," Marcus continued, "we went back to the apartment she was staying at and...well, never came out again except to eat and run occasionally."

"God. That's so romantic."

"Is it?" Marcus laughed when Heather jabbed his side.

"Of course it is, silly." She turned back to Lora. "He likes to pretend he's all manly, but he's the most romantic guy I've ever met."

Marcus changed the subject. "Is Dad angry?"

Lora's face fell. That was an understatement. "He was very concerned."

"I didn't mean to worry you both. I just got carried away. I'm sure you remember what it was like."

Lora smiled again. "I do." She sighed. "It was so long ago… I miss those days. Enjoy them while you can."

"I hope the feeling never ends."

"It won't last in the same intensity forever, but if you work hard, you can keep your relationship strong for many years." Lora glanced down at her lap, wringing her hands. The woman hadn't worked hard. Or her mate hadn't.

Heather suspected in the early days her mate had been as smitten as Marcus. And then Lora's father lured him down a horrific path.

"Have you been by your house?"

"No." Marcus shook his head. "I hope it's still standing. We came straight here. We'll go there next. I was such an ass, I didn't even call my employer. I bet they were livid when I stopped showing up for work."

"Yeah. You're father called them to see if they'd seen you. You were supposed to come to dinner that Sunday afternoon. When you didn't show up, we panicked. Your father looked for you everywhere. In fact your grandfather was here too. They both searched for days.

You never came home. And when they confirmed you never showed up for work, we didn't know what to think."

"Why was Grandpa here?"

Good one, Marcus.

Lora paused. Clearly she wasn't the one who intended to share the details of that Sunday afternoon. That was the men's job. "Oh, he has some project he wanted to invite you to participate in. Something with work."

"Huh. That's weird," Marcus said.

Yeah, about as weird as the way she stated it. Heather fought not to react to the woman's words.

"Yeah." She waved a hand as if to dismiss the idea. "Don't worry about it now. You're home, and that's what matters. You're staying, right?"

"Well, we need to go to Oregon right away and visit with Heather's parents. We haven't decided what to do after that yet."

The front door opened, startling Heather, and apparently Marcus also, because he whipped his head around as though he expected an ambush. She grabbed his arm tighter to keep him from jumping out of his seat.

The man who entered froze on the spot, his brow furrowed. "Son." He didn't step forward. "I wondered whose car was in the driveway. Where have you been?"

Not, hello... So good to see you... Oh, look, you've found your mate... We missed you so much... Just son. Heather held her breath, watching the man's reaction closely.

Marcus stood, but his thigh still touched Heather's.

Thank God. She needed his touch to ground her. "Dad. This is Heather. My mate." He turned toward her and took her hand to pull her up next to him. If not for his assistance, her wobbly legs might have given way.

Carl Cunningham turned his gaze toward her, his brow still furrowed as though he hadn't noticed her presence or the distinct scent of a newly mated couple. Finally, he nodded. "You mated." He stated the obvious with a certain amount of disappointment in his voice.

Lora stood to approach her husband, tentatively. "Isn't it wonderful?" she asked.

Heather got the distinct impression Lora was used to placating Carl. The man looked like he might blow steam any minute. Nothing on his face registered relief that his only child had returned from being missing.

Slowly, as Carl gazed absently at his mate, he snapped out of it. He jerked his face back to Marcus, and then Heather. "Welcome," he stated, belatedly. The initial reaction wasn't lost on any of them. Least of all Heather, who fought hard to keep from trembling.

Marcus lowered them both down onto their seats again, much to Heather's relief. "We were just telling Mom how we met last month and what we've been doing. She said you were worried. I'm sorry. I could think of nothing but my mate for weeks. It was rude. I apologize."

Heather wondered if Carl would stand there all night or perhaps take a seat.

"Well, you're here now. I suppose that's what matters." Carl stepped farther into the room and plopped onto an armchair as though completely deflated after holding vigil for his lost son for all twenty-seven days. Heather cringed at the irony. The man had held vigil for Marcus, but not for altruistic reasons. There was no love in his eyes. No hug. Not even a handshake. Just relief his son had returned. Most likely so good old Granddad would be placated.

"I'll start dinner." Lora stepped toward the kitchen, but Marcus stopped her.

"Mom. No. Don't. We can't stay. I need to get to my place and take care of the cobwebs and dead plants."

"Oh. You must stay. You just got here." She hesitated.

Marcus shook his head. "Next time, Mom. Not tonight. It took all my self-control to come for a visit. I'm not ready to share Heather for that long yet."

Heather wanted to kiss him for insisting. If they had to stay much longer, she wasn't sure she could keep up the act. The bile that had risen in her throat since the arrival of his father was threatening a revolt. In fact, she gripped his thigh with one hand until her knuckles hurt. She wasn't aware she was doing it until he set his hand on top of hers and loosened her grip.

As if to punctuate his words, he took her cheek in his other hand and kissed her. And then he rubbed his nose against hers.

She would have laughed at the totally ridiculous gesture not remotely like her Marcus if the situation hadn't been so dire and serious.

"Your grandfather was looking for you." Ah, so Carl wasn't going to waste any time.

"That's what Mom said. Is he okay? He isn't sick or something is he?" Marcus pasted a worried expression on his face. He was going to win an Emmy before this was all said and done.

Carl shifted his gaze toward Lora as if to admonish her for speaking a word of the conversation before he arrived. He narrowed his eyes and sent her a glare.

Lora smiled, but her hand flew to her throat. "I was just telling Marcus that Dad has some sort of business proposition for him."

Carl didn't move for a second, and Heather hoped he didn't beat the woman as soon as they were alone again. Finally, he shifted his gaze back to Marcus. "Melvin has a very enterprising business in Minnesota. He came to offer you a position."

"He needs a contractor?"

Heather could have beamed. Marcus was so convincing. After all, since Marcus was a contractor, why else would his grandfather be requesting his services?

Carl hesitated. "Not exactly. I'll let him explain. He's been as worried as we have since your disappearance. I'm sure he'll want to see you right away. I'll call him this evening." Carl fingered the arm of the chair, stroking it with the tips of his fingers.

Heather imagined him itching to pull his cell out and make that call posthaste.

"Well, I *am* out of a job..." Marcus rubbed his chin. He turned toward Heather. "Maybe this is the sort of opportunity we need, honey."

Heather smiled. Was it too strained? She didn't feel half as confident in her acting ability as the show she was watching her fantastic mate perform. "You should look into it." She turned toward Carl. "Minnesota, you said? I've never been there. I hear it's beautiful."

"Oh. I, uh…" Carl swallowed. He hadn't counted on Heather accompanying his son anywhere. She knew that, but it would be unnatural for Marcus to insinuate he was going to leave her and move to Minnesota even for a day.

Marcus interrupted to create a divergence. He set his forehead on hers. "I'll talk to him. Maybe I could call him myself tomorrow." He turned back to his father.

"Oh, well, I'm sure he'll come here in person. He's got lots of good ideas. And I know he'll be anxious for you to get started." Carl swallowed. "You've been gone so long."

"It sounds like an excellent opportunity and a change in pace. I hope he didn't find someone else."

Carl shook his head. "He really wanted you to have the job. He wanted to keep it in the family."

"Excellent." Marcus grinned as though he'd won the lottery instead of a trip to a medical facility in God-knew-where Minnesota where he would be lucky if he wasn't killed or in any way tortured.

Heather shivered, and Marcus took the cue thankfully to get out of Dodge before she lost it. He stood abruptly and hauled her next to him, putting his arm around her in support, his grip on her shoulder firmer than anyone was aware of. "Well, we've got to go. I want to get back to the house before it's dark to give it a good inspection."

Carl stood also, as did Lora.

Carl stepped toward the front door, blocking it.

For a heartbeat, Heather worried the man wouldn't let them leave, but then he stepped to one side and opened the door. "Come by in the morning, okay? I'll speak to Melvin tonight."

"Excellent. Thanks, Dad. That's a huge weight off my shoulders. At least now I won't have to worry about how to feed my mate now that I've blown through my savings acting like a love-struck idiot for a month."

Carl didn't smile, but his shoulders relaxed marginally. The important thing was for the man to buy the idea Marcus and Heather weren't a flight risk this evening.

As Marcus led Heather onto the front porch, Lora said good-bye. A new tear formed in her eye as Heather glanced back to see her in the doorway.

The moment Heather turned toward the car again and landed on solid ground at the bottom of the steps, she exhaled slowly. She couldn't get away from the house fast enough. And she ached for her mate, for all the years he'd endured under that roof, even if he hadn't known what his grandfather planned for him on the side most of his childhood. It still rankled. And she wanted to go someplace where she could hold him.

He had to be reeling from the shock. Even knowing everything that occurred in the last hour had been exactly as expected, it didn't change the fact Marcus's parents had betrayed him. That confirmation would make anyone freak out. Heather didn't believe Lora knew much about her father's plans at all, and she doubted Carl knew the entire story either, but it felt as though they'd sold their only child to the devil himself.

CHAPTER 10

Marcus drove. He didn't say a word for several minutes, keeping both hands on the steering wheel and his eyes on the road. He couldn't reach out and touch Heather yet. He felt dirty somehow, and until he purged himself of the filth that made up his entire life, he couldn't face her.

He needed a run. He hoped she would be okay with that.

When she spoke, she startled him. Her soft voice interrupted his pity party. "How far is it to your house?"

He glanced at her, and some of the anger dissipated. No matter what a son of a bitch his father was or how browbeaten his mother, he had Heather and the rest of their lives after this was all over. Even one day with her would make up for anything in his past. It already had. He took her hand. "We aren't going to my place."

"Why?"

"Because I wouldn't be able to rest one second in that place. If I never see it again, I'll be fine with that.

Few things are of any value to me there, anyway. Whatever I need, I'll send someone from NAR in to get later."

Heather inched closer to him and set a hand on his arm. Instantly he calmed, wondering why he'd avoided touching her in the first place. "NAR has the place surrounded, you know. It isn't as though someone could kidnap you from your home in the night. Besides, if you moved an inch, NAR would track you and tail you to the end of the Earth."

He knew that, intellectually, but nevertheless his stomach threatened to toss his lunch if he went home. NAR had shifters everywhere. They were undoubtedly tailing him even now in an effort to stay close. They would watch his parents' home and his own home tonight, in case anything didn't go exactly as planned.

Chip or no chip, Marcus didn't relish the idea of being kidnapped and taken to Minnesota against his will.

No. What he needed was to be convincing enough he was eager and willing to take the "job" on his own without coercing. It was the only way to ensure he had control over his communication with the outside. He knew the window would be limited. If his grandfather really did intend to conduct medical experiments on him to alter his DNA, as soon as that came to light, his world would be cut off.

He looked at Heather again and swallowed. She'd be alone, perhaps never to see him again. Or at least not the same him he'd been before the alterations his own kin had planned.

He couldn't let that happen. And he wouldn't risk it by returning to his house.

Instead he drove around in strange patterns for a while and then left town, heading for a hotel two towns over. It wasn't going to be far enough to allow him to let his guard down completely, but at least he might be able to stop the shaking.

After a run. And a shower. In that order.

Heather set her head on his shoulder.

He was glad she didn't say anything placating because nothing she could say would alleviate his concerns. They were valid. He knew good and well he'd made this bed himself, but there had been no other choice. He was committed, but that didn't make it any easier.

They drove miles past the town he wanted to stay in. He pulled off onto a side road and hid the car in a grove of trees a distance from the highway. "I need to run," he said as he cut the engine.

Heather nodded against him. "It's a good plan."

He opened his door and helped her slide out on his side. He took her face in his hands. It was dark, but he could see her perfectly. "I love you. You did beautifully back there."

She smiled. "You did too. Deserving of an Academy Award." She kissed him and then stepped back and held his gaze as she stripped from her clothes.

He knew she was trying to distract him from himself, and it was working. She could do anything she wanted as long as she looked at him like that and never stopped.

Marcus hesitated. He considered forgoing the run and fucking his mate hard on the hood of the car instead. The pent up frustration would dissipate just as easily if not quicker. But she deserved better. She deserved his full attention directed at her because he craved her, not because he needed a fuck.

And besides, until he had a shower to wash away the stench of betrayal from his parents' home, he couldn't picture himself pushing his cock into his sexy mate's body.

Firm in his decision, Marcus stripped himself of his own clothes moments behind Heather and shifted on her heels. Bless her for going along with his innate urge to take his natural form and not just pacify him but join him.

Marcus set off at a slow pace at first, fighting the need to run harder and risk losing his mate in his wake or causing her to run too hard for her size. But Heather surprised him, taking off ahead of him at a breakneck pace and glancing back with a twinkle in her eye that said, "Aren't you coming, wolfboy?"

If he could have chuckled in wolf form, he would have. Instead he had to content himself with knowing he was the luckiest bastard alive to have found Heather.

Two hours later, they had run themselves to exhaustion, eaten at a diner near the hotel, and called NAR to fill them in on what transpired at his parents' house. They checked into a room on the third floor. Marcus wished they could have stayed on the twenty-ninth floor, but the highest high-rise in this small town only extended to three floors. The farther he was from the filth that could be lurking on the street, the better.

As if she'd read his mind, Heather took his hand and lured him toward the room's king-sized bed, her ass shaking seductively in front of him. "Stop worrying. We're totally safe here. I'm sure even NAR was lost a few times on the way."

He rolled his shoulders as his mate distracted him with a second strip tease. This time he intended to take full advantage of her nudity, and he quickly removed his own clothing to drop it on the floor. "Let's get in the shower. I can smell my parents' house on my clothes. I might have to burn them."

She nodded and turned for the bathroom, dropping another garment every few feet along the way. "We *could* burn our clothes if it will make you feel better." She knew just what to say to lighten the mood. "Or we could forget the trip down memory lane altogether, and I could take your mind off things in a more entertaining fashion." She turned in the doorway and waggled her eyebrows. The words she uttered next were the exact one's he'd imagined in the woods earlier. "Are you coming, wolfboy?"

Marcus lunged at her, pinning her to the vanity in the tiny bathroom when she stepped back. He took her lips in a deep kiss. She tasted of the outdoors and the sweetener she'd put in her tea at dinner. He wanted to consume her. And he would. As soon as they were clean.

Still kissing her, he reached under her ass and lifted

her against his body. She wrapped her legs around him, and he carried her to the shower.

He waited until they were inside, and he plastered her against the tile with her legs still gripped around his waist to turn on the water.

She yelped at the instantly cold waterfall running over her body.

The water grew warmer quickly. Marcus was almost disappointed as he reached for the knob to turn down the temperature as it got too hot. Returning his gaze to his mate, he tucked his fingers back under her ass and reached farther until he could pull her pussy open with his middle fingers and press them toward her center.

She squirmed again, this time to dislodge him rather than avoid the water.

He set her down slowly, hating when his cock lost the intense direct contact. It bobbed in front of him, and Heather reached with one hand to stroke the tip.

He moaned and then stepped from her grasp and turned her around to face the wall.

A shiver wracked her body, one he could feel clear through his own at such close proximity. He wanted to stroke his finger through her pussy again, but he didn't dare. She'd likely come from that simple contact, and he wanted her to wait while he pampered her body in the shower.

Marcus reached for the shampoo and poured it in his hand. When he set his palms on her red curls and massaged her scalp, she tipped her head back on a moan. "That feels so good."

He nudged her legs apart with one of his and planted

his foot between them. Massaging her head longer than necessary was easy. The longer he stayed in the shower and stared at his mate's sexy ass, the longer he could avoid reality and concentrate on the mate he'd met only a few days ago, whom he was in no way done exploring. Especially knowing there was always the chance he would never see her again.

He hadn't said as much out loud at any point in the planning, but inside he knew what his grandfather was capable of. He'd been the recipient of years of experimental drugs. The man no more loved him and cared about his wellbeing than a blade of grass under his shoe. Visiting his parents that evening confirmed his fears. No blood relation of his would be a champion in his court. His father was clearly in cahoots with his crazy grandfather, and his mother was spineless.

Slipping his fingers through Heather's long hair and down her body, he rubbed the suds from the shampoo across her back. Reluctantly, he released her skin to grab the bar of soap. He lathered his hands and then reached around to cup her breasts and pinch her nipples between his slippery fingers.

Heather swayed forward. She planted her hands on the tile wall to steady herself.

Marcus wrapped one hand around a breast and smoothed the other down her body. He parted her folds and stroked her lower lips.

Heather lifted up on tiptoes.

Marcus took the opportunity to press his knee tighter between her legs. His cock landed on her back though, and he gritted his teeth to keep from reacting.

He took a deep breath, but he was too far gone to avoid taking her. Instead, he spun her around and lifted her, sliding her back against the wall. "Wrap your legs around me again." As she did so, he settled her on his cock.

Her hands gripped his shoulders as she gasped.

"Do you know what you do to me?" he gritted out.

She nodded, her face leaning in until she kissed him.

With only his hands as leverage, he lifted her and set her back down, groaning at the feel of her pussy around his cock, all slippery and wet. He gripped her ass with both hands and inched them toward her puckered hole.

Heather squirmed, but he held her firm as he pressed a middle finger into her while she remained lodged on his cock. "You okay?"

She moaned, her eyes closing halfway. "More than."

He held her butt cheeks, keeping his finger inside her as he increased the speed and pumped into her. His balls drew up tight as he held her gaze, noting the glazed look in her eyes. He loved the way her lips parted when they had sex.

Heather's legs stiffened around him, letting him know she was close. To deny her would be futile.

Marcus pumped faster. "Come, baby. I want to feel your pussy gripping my cock when I come."

Without hesitation, her orgasm swept through her.

Marcus held back for only a moment and then followed her over the edge as she set her forehead on his shoulder, gasping for air.

They stayed that way for several minutes. Marcus

eased his finger out of her and massaged her ass. "You're so amazing."

"You aren't too bad yourself." She grinned as she lifted her face.

Marcus kissed her deeply, his tongue sliding in to tangle with hers. He'd do anything to put off the inevitable and avoid tomorrow.

∼

Heather awoke to the sound of the shower running again. Every muscle in her body ached pleasantly from sex in more positions than she could have dreamed. She stretched. They hadn't slept more than a few hours, making love until nearly dawn.

The water shut off, and she rolled onto her side to watch as her mate appeared in the doorway.

He smiled. "I tried not to wake you."

"Why?" She forced herself to push to a sitting position and swing her legs over the side of the bed. "It's not like you were going to leave without me." She stood, but when he hesitated, she narrowed her gaze at him. "Right?"

He exhaled. "I wish I could. I hate taking you back over to my parents."

"But you have to. What time are we leaving?" She padded past him, aiming for the shower herself.

"My dad texted me several times last night to make sure we were there by ten. Apparently my grandfather is flying in this morning. I think I'm meant to be honored by the man's concern and willingness to give me such a wonderful opportunity." Sarcasm oozed from Marcus as he reached for a comb and pushed it through his hair roughly.

Heather wrapped her arms around him from behind after she flipped the water back on. She wanted to say everything would be fine, but she didn't feel it. She was scared shitless. And she knew he would never admit it out loud, but he was too. Instead, she trailed kisses across his shoulder blades and reluctantly released him to get in the shower.

Marcus turned around. She could feel his gaze on her as she let the water fall over her head. "We sure take a lot of showers." She peered through the glass door at him.

He leaned against the vanity, legs crossed at the ankles, hands gripping the countertop on both sides of his narrow waist.

Heather fought to stay in the shower and not attack him. He was that sexy. She closed her eyes as she washed, trying to forget he stared at her. It would do no good to insist he leave.

When she finished, he handed her a towel. "Do you know how badly I want to take you back to bed?" His gaze roamed down her body, drawing out a flush in its wake.

"Yes." Her voice was hoarse. She dried quickly as Marcus rounded behind her.

"Stand still, baby."

She didn't know what he had in mind, but was pleasantly surprised to find he held her comb and proceeded to work through her tangled locks as she watched in the mirror. His gentle hands took their time, and she tried not to fidget as she stood there, a slight chill making her nipples pucker.

He leaned forward and kissed the top of her head as he finished.

She spun around to face him, set her hands on his chest, and held his gaze. "You're so strong. I'm so proud of you."

He swallowed as he wrapped his arms around her. "And I of you, baby."

Reluctantly she released him. They dressed quickly and checked out of the hotel before nine, intent on grabbing some breakfast on the way back to his parents'.

"Did you tell NAR what our plans are for this morning?"

"Yeah. I texted them earlier before you were up. They'll be on watch."

At ten sharp they pulled up outside the small house, noting the extra car in the driveway.

Marcus gripped the steering wheel and took a deep breath. "The man is nothing if not punctual. This is going to be the hardest thing I've ever done. I'm not an actor."

"You can do it. You have to. And I'll be right next to you."

He turned toward her. "Until you aren't." He took her hand. "Please make sure you're always with someone from NAR when this goes down. I'm assuming I'll go with my grandfather, and you'll take this rental as though leaving to visit your parents. Alex will meet you someplace nearby."

"I know. I've got it memorized." They'd discussed this a dozen times in the last two days. "Don't worry about me. I'll be fine. Concentrate on keeping *you* alive. Please." She pleaded with him. "I—"

Before she could say anything, Marcus kissed her and then closed her mouth with a hand on her chin. "Don't say it." He climbed out of the car.

Heather stepped out on her side and rounded the hood to take his hand.

The front door opened before they reached the steps. Carl stepped out. He looked relieved. His shoulders fell as he motioned for them to enter. "I was worried about you two."

Heather doubted that. But she waited for the reason.

"Why?" Marcus asked. "We said we'd be here at ten. It's ten now."

"Where did you go last night? You weren't at your house," Carl asked.

Heather tried to hide the tremble creeping up her neck. Marcus had been right. The man had followed them, or at least driven over to make sure they were actually home. Thank God they hadn't stayed there. The creepiness factor alone made her cringe again.

"Oh. That," Marcus began in his totally calm rehearsed voice. "I decided the place needed a good cleaning before it would be habitable." He chuckled, though Heather knew he didn't feel one bit of humor. "We got a hotel."

Carl nodded as though he didn't really care what the answer was as long as they were there now.

The first thing Heather noticed as she entered the house was how small Melvin Cunningham was. She'd expected a giant, towering, muscular man, considering what he'd orchestrated to the detriment of the entire shifter population.

Instead she found herself staring at an ailing man who appeared more frail than fit. His expression was stern, his brow furrowed. And he notably didn't stand from where he sat in an armchair in the Cunningham living room.

"Marcus." He nodded as they entered.

"Grandfather." Marcus took a seat on the couch, the same place he'd sat yesterday, keeping a tight grip on Heather.

Her hand hurt, but she wasn't about to deflect his attention. If it grounded him and gave him comfort, she would do anything.

"So, Dad tells me you have a business proposition."

"I do indeed. Though I do wish you hadn't disappeared for a month." He narrowed his gaze in admonishment.

Heather flinched, surprised at the audacity of the man to reprimand his grandson before tossing him to the lions.

Marcus grinned, as though he hadn't noticed the castigation, and looked down at Heather. "I'm sure you've heard the reason for my disappearing act. This is Heather. My mate."

"Nice to meet you," Heather managed through the lump in her throat threatening to choke her to death.

Melvin merely nodded toward her as though she were hardly more than a blip on his radar. Heather held her breath, praying he didn't recognize her. Did the man have a pile of photos of the twelve women he'd arranged to have kidnapped and drugged?

At last Cunningham resumed his perusal of Marcus. He cleared his throat and continued. "As I'm sure your parents mentioned, I own a facility in Minnesota, and since you're my only descendant, I want to bring you into the fold."

Heather exhaled long and slow as he redirected his attention to Marcus, not showing any sign of knowing who she was. She noted how the man carefully didn't mention what sort of facility his business was. She'd been briefed on the place. NAR had gathered information from a few sources, both helpful and reluctant. Daniel Spencer's mate had spent some time at the facility also. Granted, she'd been in a drug-induced haze most of the time, but she did know enough to verify it was a medical facility of sorts.

The head elder, Ralph Jerard, was certain the facility was the location responsible for the conversion of dozens of shifters into superwolves through DNA alteration.

Fortunately, it didn't seem it was going to take any convincing to get Melvin-the-Asswipe to lead Marcus straight to the location. As long as Marcus arrived at the facility, NAR would be hot on his heels in pursuit. That part was easy. With the tracking device, Marcus didn't even need to call with coordinates.

Beating the Romulus at their own game by implanting a GPS tracker in Marcus in the same way the Romulus had tracked several of the kidnapped women would have been comical if it weren't so risky.

Heather dug her nails into Marcus's hand.

"That's what I've heard." Marcus nodded. "Good timing. I lost my job when I fled town with my mate. I could use a relocation. What sort of work do you have in mind? Do you need some construction?"

Melvin shook his head. "No. Nothing like that. It's a research facility. You'll be learning the business so that eventually you can take over for me."

Marcus gasped, feigning shock. "Take over? But I don't even know what you do."

"You'll learn. You're a bright young man." Melvin turned to glance at Heather, giving her the creeps. "I'm sure your new mate would appreciate the steady work."

Marcus turned to look at Heather also. "I think Heather would like me to get a job ASAP." He chuckled and nudged her playfully. "She likes nice things, and I've been negligent since we met."

She fought to avoid rolling her eyes, hoping he hadn't laid it on too thick. *Nice things, my ass.* She wouldn't care if she never had anything but enough to eat and drink for the rest of her life as long as she had Marcus. Even a roof was overrated. They could always shift in the woods if they needed. She tried not to smile at the idea.

Melvin narrowed his gaze again. "She needs to stay

here for the time being. I'm afraid the accommodations aren't up to par yet. You'll be living inside the compound at first. It's no place for a woman."

That Heather didn't jump from the couch and tell Melvin where the fuck to go and take his antiquated ideas about women was a testament to her ability as said woman to hold her calm. Besides, what he meant was the facility was no place for a woman who wasn't part of his experiment. The main hitch in this entire plan had been the concern Melvin might suggest Heather come also. In that case, Marcus insisted he would have bailed entirely. No way would he take her into the place blind. He'd made that clear on more than one occasion.

So, while Melvin's words cut to the quick and degraded women in general, Heather was relieved to hear he didn't intend for her to join them.

Marcus frowned. "I'm not ready to separate from my mate yet. I'm sure you can understand that. And you haven't told me what your compound is for. What kind of research?"

Heather bit her lip. As much as she knew Marcus hated to harp on the question, it would seem too convenient if he didn't inquire. Marcus hadn't been known for his easy acquiescence in things in the past. He added to his statement with the planned explanation for his willingness.

"Medical research." Melvin fidgeted as he explained. "We're working on improving the life-expectancy of our species." He beamed.

Heather cringed. *Life expectancy. Right.* That's what

he thought was the best explanation for his secret compound where wolves were undergoing DNA transformation in order to become super fighting machines? She wondered, not for the first time, if anyone at the "compound" was there of their own free will.

Marcus paused a moment, pretending to consider his grandfather's proposal. "Heather needs to go to Oregon and visit her parents. She's been gone for a while. Right, honey?" He turned toward her.

"Aren't you going to come with me?" She pouted enough to be believable.

Melvin interrupted. "I'm afraid I'll need you rather urgently, my boy. There's no time for dawdling on vacation. You'll have to forgo the trip to Oregon and head straight with me to Minnesota to assume the position."

Marcus blew out a breath and stared down at Heather. "Will you be okay without me for a bit? I promise I'll accompany you to Oregon as soon as I can break away from my job. This sounds like an opportunity we shouldn't pass up."

Feigning reluctance, she nodded. "Soon, I hope." She let her shoulders fall. "My mother will be so disappointed." She turned toward Lora, who hadn't spoken a single syllable since they'd arrived. "You know how mothers feel about their kids growing up and mating." She rolled her eyes.

Lora gave a faint smile and nodded.

Carl, who remained standing and was the only one in the room pacing the floor, spoke again. "Mated or not, you can't pass up this opportunity, Marcus. Heather will have to wait for you to get settled and then come out and join you when you've found appropriate housing."

Heather wondered briefly if Marcus's parents knew the extent of what was happening at the compound in Minnesota. Were they so oblivious they believed Heather would actually be permitted to reunite with her mate in a few weeks? God, how she wanted that to be the case. The alternative was so unimaginable she couldn't face it head on.

What parents would be in favor of donating their only child to some strange science experiment, knowing he would be forever altered or killed in the process? A chill shook her frame.

Marcus pretended to consider the proposition some more, setting his free hand on his chin and stroking it. "When would you need me?"

"Right now, son. Today. A month ago." Carl leaned forward, setting his hands on the back of a vacant chair.

Marcus furrowed his brow. He sighed. "Honey?"

Heather easily conjured up a few tears to glisten her eyes. "I guess it's for the best. I'll go see my parents and catch up with you as soon as possible."

Marcus turned back to face Melvin. "I'd need to pack some things."

"Do you always have to be so disagreeable, Marcus?" Carl stood once more, his voice lifting as he paced.

Heather startled at his outburst. She gripped Marcus's arm, wondering who was the most deranged, Melvin or Carl.

Melvin held up a hand. For a frail man, he could certainly put Carl in his place fast. Heather almost chuckled. "I'll escort the boy to his home to gather his things. Let's not be unreasonable, Carl. He needs clothing, after all."

Heather doubted Marcus needed any clothing for whatever Melvin had in mind.

Carl headed for the front door and opened it. "Well, let's go. Time's a wasting."

"Will we be flying?" Marcus asked.

Melvin shook his head. "No. We can drive from here. You can manage, right? I don't drive as often as I used to at my age."

"Of course." Marcus's pulse steadied at the news. Heather squeezed his hand. Neither of them wanted Marcus to fly anywhere. It would cause them to lose track of him for a while in the air. On the ground, members of NAR could stay on his heels the entire trip.

Everyone stood.

Marcus led Heather out the door. "I'll drive Heather to my place. Can you follow us, Dad? I'd like a few minutes with my mate before we separate. You can understand." He didn't ask. He told.

Carl nodded. "We'll be right behind you."

Marcus pointed at the car in front of the house. "Yours?" he asked his grandfather.

"A rental. We'll be taking it. You can leave yours for your mate."

"Also a rental." He turned to Heather. "You can turn it in at the airport when you head to Oregon. I wish we had time for me to take you to the airport myself, but it seems my grandfather's in a hurry." He chuckled and glanced over at the rest of his family getting in his grandfather's rental car.

"I'll be fine. I've flown many times." She smiled, but it was forced to the point of painful.

When they were safely in the car with the doors closed, Heather exhaled. "I think I held my breath the entire time."

"Me too, baby. I was sweating bullets. I hope I didn't hurt your hand. I couldn't keep from squeezing it." He picked it up and kissed her knuckles after he started the ignition.

"I'm still shaking."

"I will be until this is all over."

"It's going to be a long drive alone in the car with your grandfather."

"No kidding."

"I wasn't expecting someone so frail. I imagined him being tall and built and domineering." Heather reached across the console to set her hand on her mate's thigh, not wanting to miss a single opportunity to touch him. She glanced out the rear window as they drove away.

Marcus must have read her mind. He lifted his other hip, pulled out a cell, and handed it to her. "Text Jerard. Tell him to have Alex pick you up at my house after we've left. Plan B."

"I didn't expect them to let you go back to the house." Heather opened the throwaway phone and texted. "I know you didn't really want to go back there."

"Yeah, I didn't expect that, either. I guess my sweet

grandfather didn't want to rock the boat and risk me not going with him willingly."

"Do you think he would have taken you by force if you hadn't agreed?"

"I'm sure of it." Marcus kept his gaze peeled on the road in every direction. His family followed close behind them, but Heather knew he was nervous about NAR following also.

"Don't worry. They're trained professionals. They won't get caught. Besides," Heather held up the phone, "I told them where we're going. And there's no chance they can lose us with the tracking device you have."

"I know. You're right." He glanced at her again. "I love you."

"I love you too." She swallowed.

"Please be careful. Don't do anything to get yourself dead."

"Same goes for you, mutt. I've grown to enjoy your company, even lying like an animal at the foot of my bed."

Marcus smiled.

Good. She'd hoped to lighten the mood a bit.

"I'm going to leave you the keys to my house and car. If anything happens…"

"It won't." She squeezed his arm. "It can't."

He nodded, and his left leg tapped rapidly on the floorboard. "I've never been so nervous in my life. Not even shifting for the first time and facing you at the Spencers' made me as nervous as this."

"I know." She couldn't agree, though. She'd been pretty fucking nervous when the Romulus kidnapped her. That week had been ten times worse than this. At least this time, NAR was in the rearview mirror, ready to jump in and save the day. She'd had no hope last time. She'd known she would die in that basement, and that had made a permanent dent in her psyche.

"I need more time."

"I know that too."

Marcus pulled into the driveway of a quaint little house. They'd only gone a few miles, as Heather had known they would. "This is it. It isn't much, but I didn't have many needs before I met you." He turned to her and took her face. "Do whatever you need to here after I leave. What's mine is yours. If it makes you feel better, go through my things."

She nodded. She would never do that, but she couldn't speak right then.

Marcus kissed her and then opened the door without breaking her gaze. "I guess we should go in and gather my shit. Unless you want me to take nothing that makes any sense, you better help me. I'm liable to stuff a rug and two potholders in my suitcase instead of clothes."

Heather got out on the other side. "I'll make sure you're adequately packed." Though she had no idea how she could do a better job than him. She knew he'd only said it to give her something to think about besides his departure.

His family pulled up behind them, and his parents exited the car. Carl had driven. Lora climbed from the back seat and stood beside the car wringing her hands.

She took Carl's arm when he stepped toward the house. "Give them some privacy, dear. They just mated."

Carl glanced down at where his mate held his arm. For a moment Heather thought the man might backhand her. He stiffened and opened his mouth. Apparently thinking better of it, he nodded. "Don't take more than a few minutes, Marcus. It's a long drive."

Melvin remained seated in the vehicle. Heather shuddered as she pictured Marcus's grandfather staring at her back as she followed Marcus to the house.

She held it together until they got inside, and then she leaned against the door and exhaled. "God, that man is intense."

Marcus turned around and pressed himself against her, flattening his palms on both sides of her head. "Leave that asshole outside so we can enjoy the last few minutes together." His lips descended as she licked hers. When he kissed her, he consumed her, making the kiss powerful enough she wouldn't soon forget the feel of his lips on hers. He cocked his head and angled to get a deeper position. His tongue teased the inside of her mouth, battling against her own as though they could remember each other's tastes longer if they could make the kiss more intense.

When he pulled back and set his forehead against hers, he was breathing heavily. His hands cupped her face. "You're the most important person in the world to me. Do you understand?"

She nodded.

"Take care of yourself," he repeated for the dozenth

time. Abruptly he stood and grabbed her hand to lead her down a short hall. He didn't say anything.

Obviously it was his bedroom. His scent lingered even after a month of absence. *Perhaps I'll stay for a while and breathe him in after he leaves.*

Heather sat on the edge of the bed and watched as Marcus grabbed a suitcase from the closet and tossed several items from every drawer into the luggage.

She smiled. He would indeed be shocked by what he'd packed later, but she couldn't manage to help. She wanted to watch him instead, memorize every move he made, the way his muscles flexed as he pushed on the contents to make more room, the way his jaw tightened as he realized he'd stuffed too many items inside.

When he finally shut the suitcase and set it on end on the floor, he stepped into her space. He hesitated, staring at her. "I want to flatten you on my bed and make love to you again."

Heather gave a brief nod. She wanted that too. It wasn't going to happen, though.

"Stay right here until I'm gone. I can't stand the idea of you watching me pull away." He inched closer, took her in his arms, and pulled her close. "Have I mentioned I love you?"

"Many times." She smiled.

He kissed her quickly and stepped back, his fingers the last part of him she had contact with as he stretched their arms out and stepped away.

She fought to hold back a gasp as their fingertips parted and her arm fell to her side.

Marcus picked up the suitcase and walked out of the room without another word.

She listened as his hastened footsteps hit the hardwood floor on the way to the front door.

She imagined him composing himself in the seconds after he stopped walking but before he opened the door.

And then, just as quickly, the door closed, and she was left in silence. She sat for several minutes in that exact spot, her eyes closed as she heard the engine of the car come to life and pull away. Marcus would drop his parents back off at home and then start the long drive to Minnesota with his grandfather. She fought to breathe properly, finally scooting back and lying on his bed. She buried her face in his pillow and inhaled his scent. Tears filled her eyes, but she didn't sob. She let them fall silently.

When the front door opened again, she didn't flinch. It would be someone from NAR. She heard Alex's voice from the front room. "Heather?"

She didn't move yet, taking in the last seconds of her time in Marcus's space.

Footsteps grew closer. They stopped. "You okay?" Alex's voice was gentle.

Heather pulled herself to sitting, brushing the moisture from her eyes. She nodded. "I will be. Let's get going. I don't want to lose him." She lifted her gaze to Alex.

He opened his mouth to say something.

"Don't even give me any bullshit about taking me along. If you thought you were going to stash me with someone and go without me, you're crazy." She stood, resolved. She wiped her hands on her jeans and straightened her spine. "I'm going with you. Don't argue with me."

Alex nodded, his mouth curving up in a half smile. "Of course you are."

CHAPTER 11

Heather stared out the window, watching the trees go by, although she realized she hadn't actually seen anything since they'd left Marcus's house. Several reserves had come to get her. Someone returned the rental car for her, and now she sped down the highway in the backseat of an average-looking, nondescript black sedan with Alex and another member of NAR, Silas.

She knew they were only miles behind Marcus, and it comforted her to know it. Alex had a constant reading on his location. They could thank the Romulus for the tip on embedding a GPS tracker in Marcus's arm. They'd inserted it beneath his armpit in the fatty tissue of his bicep, though where they managed to find fatty anything on Marcus she didn't know. But that's what the man who'd inserted the chip had said.

They drove for three hours before Marcus stopped moving, undoubtedly to get lunch. Heather was antsy the entire time they were stopped. They pulled over at a gas station, filled the tank, and proceeded to pretend to study a map while they waited for Marcus to move again.

Heather's entourage grabbed sandwiches from the convenience center. Heather couldn't swallow even a sip of water.

"You have to eat something, Heather," Alex said. "Marcus will kill me if I don't take good care of you." He tried to smile. Or maybe he actually did. But she was zoned and unable to pick up sarcasm with ease.

"I will. But not now. Don't worry. I won't waste away."

As soon as Alex declared, "They're on the move again," they climbed back in the car and kept going.

Alex texted the other members of NAR every time they stopped and then resumed the chase, letting them know where they were and any time they changed highways.

Jerard was in one of the other cars. Heather was impressed the elder was going with them.

Marcus had not taken his cell phone. He'd intentionally left it behind with Heather. That way she would have access to all his contacts, and he would have one thing less to worry about having confiscated from him upon arrival.

Heather couldn't imagine the amount of stress he was feeling trapped in a car with his godforsaken grandfather, who had nothing but bad intentions with regard to his only grandchild.

She tried to rest her eyes for a while, but every time she closed them, she pictured herself in that basement for the longest week of her life. In the month since her rescue, she'd come a long way toward healing, but it all came back to her now that Marcus was about to face such an unknown fate.

Alex pulled over at another gas station several hours later. Heather was about to wet her pants by then, but she hadn't dared ask to stop. Putting even an extra half mile between her and Marcus made her uneasy.

"They must have stopped for gas. We'll fill up here ourselves and use the facilities. If either of you needs anything, go ahead and grab it. Who knows how much farther we have to go." Alex stretched as he stepped from the car.

Heather and Silas headed inside and returned quickly. Silas had grabbed snacks and drinks. He passed a Gatorade to Heather. "You at least need something in you." He smiled warmly. "I know your stomach must be ready to revolt, but at least drink. When we see Marcus again, he's going to be livid enough we let you come with us. If he finds out we didn't feed you, he'll have a conniption."

Heather took the yellow drink and got back in the car. Silas was right, but she was afraid she would need to vomit if she drank. Bile stayed high in her throat, threatening to erupt at the slightest provocation.

The phone rang as they pulled back on the highway, making Heather jump in her seat.

Alex answered it on Bluetooth. "Jerard."

Heather exhaled. The leader of the free shifters, as she'd come to think of him, spoke. "Where are you?"

"Middle of nowhere, Minnesota, best I can tell," Alex

responded jokingly. "We went through Minneapolis and then headed northwest on Highway 94 about an hour ago."

"Not having any trouble following the tracking device?"

"No. And it's still moving north. I'll let you know as soon as we stop."

"Good. Keep me informed. I'm about thirty minutes behind you." Jerard cut the connection.

"Are we there yet?" Heather said to lighten the mood, more for herself perhaps than the others.

"Almost." Alex smiled at her in the rearview mirror.

It was another hour before the GPS stopped moving. Heather had been watching the red dot on the black box sitting on the dashboard for so long her eyes hurt. When it stopped, she sat forward.

Silas pulled off the road about half a minute later. "We're only about a half mile from Marcus. Let's wait for backup, and then we'll spread out and see what the area looks like. We have about five hours of daylight left." He pulled his cell out and dialed. "Jerard. We stopped. We're only a few miles from North Dakota. We'll wait here for the rest of you to arrive and then scan the area. It looks like Marcus turned right just ahead of where we are, so that means he went about a half mile off the highway."

"Got it. Inform the others. We'll see you soon."

Alex texted everyone else.

Heather wanted to shift and run toward her mate. Her body called to act. She had to fight her inner wolf to keep it at bay. Now was no time to shift. In human form they could approach and get a better view of the facility. Shifters could scent other shifters far easier in their natural form than when they took the shape of men and women. The last thing they wanted was to attract attention and cause any suspicion from the Romulus.

They didn't even know how many men were at this research center yet. Until they knew for sure what they were up against, Heather knew no one was going to do anything rash.

Heather paced next to the car while they waited for the rest of their party to arrive. Three more vehicles pulled off the highway half an hour later. They easily slid deep into the tall grass and down a short decline in the embankment to keep the cars out of sight.

Twelve reserves plus the two men Heather arrived with pulled out maps and studied the precise location of Marcus's chip.

Jerard leaned over. "Whatever the place is, it's not on any map."

"Could we pull it up with a satellite image?" Silas asked.

"Probably, but not as quickly as we'd like and not without creating suspicion. I don't have those kinds of connections in the human world." Jerard stepped back. "Though it's seeming more and more like we're going to need them."

Heather leaned against one of the cars. The fact shifters were considering revealing themselves to the outside was huge. She never expected to see something like this in her lifetime.

Although according to what Marcus heard from his grandfather last month, humans were already informed. At least whoever was funding the Romulus. And whoever was funding the Romulus was on the side of evil.

"Okay, let's spread out and surround the place. Silence your phones and text when anyone sees anything worth noting." Alex pointed at groups of men and paired them off. "Heather, you're with me and Silas."

Thank God they didn't intend to leave her behind. She'd have given them the riot act.

~

Marcus was exhausted. The drive alone would have made him tired under any ordinary circumstances, but when he factored in the old man next to him for the last eight hours, he was about to stab himself. The man yammered incessantly about the importance of family and the need to ensure the continuity of their species.

Undoubtedly his aim had been to manipulate Marcus into being more receptive to whatever experiments the man was conducting at his medical facility.

When Melvin was convinced he had Marcus sufficiently lured into his net, he moved on to the value of making wolves stronger and more self-sufficient so no threat from humans or any other species on Earth would be insurmountable to them.

Marcus listened closely, even though he would have

rather tuned the man out hours ago. He needed to hear everything to be the most informed and to gather the most intel for NAR.

Finally, Melvin had fallen asleep for a while, and Marcus hadn't dared make a single noise or even turn on the radio, relishing the silence and praying the man took the longest afternoon nap possible.

His grandfather awoke as though on cue and directed Marcus the last few miles to the compound, as he referred to the place.

Marcus's first impression was shock at the size of the facility. He'd imagined a white, hospital-like building with several stories. Instead he faced a single-story spread painted a deep green that covered so much area it had to be at least twenty-thousand square feet. And that didn't begin to consider how far underground it extended. The building blended in with the foliage with its green coloring, and Marcus was certain it was no accident.

When he emerged from the car and stretched his legs, his grandfather did the same on the other side. Marcus didn't round the car to aid the man. For one, he'd rather not get so close, and for two, Melvin wasn't the sort of character to take kindly to the assumption he required assistance.

Marcus followed his grandfather through an ordinary door on the side of the building. He wondered if it were the front entrance or a random side door. He saw no evidence to indicate any particular part of the building was a welcoming front.

The minute they entered, Marcus understood where

he got the impression the building would be white. It had been Allison Watkins, Daniel's mate, who informed NAR she remembered a stark white medical setting. Indeed the inside was completely white, from the ceiling tiles to the floor.

Marcus tried to hide his shock as he followed his grandfather down a long hall and into an office. Melvin rounded a desk and plopped down, pushing a button on the phone to the right. "Cathy, please bring us some sandwiches and some water."

"Yes, sir," replied the soft voice on the other end. "Right away." Melvin looked up and then gestured to a chair in front of the desk. "Are you just going to stand there? Sit."

Marcus lowered onto the chair, even though he would have rather remained standing. His butt hurt from sitting for so long, and his nerves were shot to hell.

Minutes later a blonde woman walked into the room carrying a tray. She set it down on the desk and scampered back out the door without a word.

Marcus kept from rolling his eyes. Of course his grandfather only had a demure, quiet woman at his beck and call.

"Eat. You must be starving. We haven't stopped since lunch." Melvin picked up a sandwich. "Then I'll show you around a little. We'll get you settled in what will be your quarters and get started first thing tomorrow."

Marcus reached for the second sandwich, wondering how he was going to swallow a single bite. He was beyond nervous by now.

At least no one has tried to inject you with anything yet. That's a plus.

Being drugged against his will was his biggest concern in this mission. If anyone slipped anything in his food or stabbed him with a needle, he could become helpless to defend himself or be of any assistance to the group of reserves he knew had the place surrounded by now.

He'd seen a man on the roof as they'd entered and assumed there were guards on the other side of the building. Melvin was cunning. He wouldn't leave himself unprotected, even out in the middle of nowhere.

What are you up to, old man?

It took herculean effort for Marcus to swallow his sandwich while maintaining an appearance of nonchalance. He started slowly, concerned about being drugged. But as minutes passed with no obvious signs of impairment, he picked up the pace. As much as he loathed the idea of eating anything in this facility, he would need the energy. He couldn't very well tell his grandfather he wasn't hungry. It wouldn't be believable.

When they finished, he waited for his grandfather to type at his computer for several minutes before the man stood. "Let's get to that tour, shall we?"

"What exactly do you do here?" Marcus asked. To do otherwise would have seemed peculiar. Even though Melvin had given him vague answers at his parents' home that morning, Marcus had nothing substantial to go on from his grandfather's explanation.

"Experiments, son." His grandfather turned to give

him a look indicating he was a moron. "It's a research facility. What else would you expect?"

At the condescending tone, Marcus decided to keep his mouth shut lest he be inclined to punch the man and ruin the hard work of NAR on the outside preparing to attack.

Melvin sped down various halls with amazing agility for a man as frail as he appeared. He pointed out mundane rooms as they went. "Restrooms. Lab. Break room." He continued down another hall and then gestured the length. "Most of the staff sleeps in the quarters on this hall."

He kept walking until he came to the third door on the left. "This one will be yours for now." He slid a key card in the slot next to the handle and pushed through to the room.

For now? What happens later?

The inside was no more than a motel room. Double bed. Bathroom. Small desk and lamp. Marcus noted his suitcase sat at the end of the bed. That meant someone had retrieved it from the car.

"Get a good night's sleep. We'll be working early tomorrow. Someone will come to collect you at six o'clock. Use the alarm." Melvin left as soon as he spoke those words, leaving Marcus both relieved and concerned at the same time.

The first thing he did was check the door he'd just come through. As he expected, it was locked. He inhaled slowly, trying to control his emotions. Of course the man wouldn't want him wandering around the facility before he'd had an opportunity to introduce him to his new fate.

"This one will be yours for now."

Those words ran over and over in his head. How long was *now*? He sure the fuck hoped it was longer than whatever time NAR needed to collect intelligence and bust down the front door.

Marcus had agreed to twenty-four hours inside before anyone moved. It would take the reserves that long to assess the manpower needed for the job and assemble the troops. It would also give Marcus the chance to gather as much information as possible. If NAR busted in too soon, they stood the chance of learning nothing of what was happening on the inside.

Marcus plopped on the bed and stared at the ceiling. He hadn't been without his mate for this long since he'd met her, and he wasn't pleased with her absence now. *Hold it together. By this time tomorrow, hopefully it will all be over, and you'll be free to enjoy Heather for the rest of your life.*

How the hell was he going to sleep? And he needed to so he would be in top shape when the door opened in the morning. He would be useless to NAR if he was a zombie in the morning.

Pulling himself up, Marcus set the alarm. *What a joke.* And then he made his way to the bathroom to shower away the ugliness of the day and brush his teeth.

When he lay back down on the bed with nothing more to do but wait, he closed his eyes and breathed in deeply. *Heather, baby, I hope you're resting better than I am tonight.* He doubted she was. But he could hope.

CHAPTER 12

Marcus was ready when the door opened in the morning. He was surprised to find his grandfather on the other side. The man motioned for him to follow.

"Is everyone locked in their rooms at night?" Being slightly antagonistic was a necessary part of the deed. If he were too willing to be led around like a trained monkey, Melvin would be suspicious. He had to keep reminding himself to question things.

"Yes. Keeps everyone safe."

"From what?" The question popped out of his mouth unbidden.

"You never know." His grandfather shrugged. "Come on. I'm going to show you some things that will blow your mind this morning."

Marcus was sure.

The first place they went was a dining hall. Dozens of shifters scurried around the buffet and ate like little robots. No one paid much attention to the newcomer. Marcus wondered if they were under the influence of some substance to keep them docile. He remembered being in a similar state at times during his teens. Was this how his grandfather ran his facility? With robotic shifters who knew nothing else?

Marcus moved down the buffet line in the dining hall, carefully selecting only the things his grandfather chose, still concerned about being drugged. He hardly tasted anything and couldn't describe it afterward if he needed to. He then followed his grandfather down several halls, trying to remember where he was and where he'd come from.

Finally they passed through two double doors and entered what looked like an emergency room. There weren't any patients waiting to be seen, but the front desk looked busy anyway. Chairs lined the walls as though they were expecting a rush of incoming patients at any moment.

Marcus hoped he wasn't the first victim of the day.

He said nothing as his grandfather led him past the staff and behind the scenes. Marcus looked both ways as they walked. Every room had someone in it on a gurney. No one appeared to be awake. Everyone had IVs attached to them, but Marcus didn't notice anything else out of the ordinary.

"Are all these people sick?" he asked. Seemed like a reasonable question.

"No. On the contrary, they're all in the best health of their lives." Melvin kept walking. "Thanks to my medical experts." *As if that explains everything.*

Marcus swallowed, fear climbing up his spine as they progressed farther into the facility. His grandfather was crazier than he'd expected. The man didn't flinch as he pushed through another set of doors.

Marcus came up short as he stopped face to face with an enormous window. At first he didn't see anything behind the window, and then he realized the room on the other side of the glass was recessed about twenty feet. He inched closer and peered below. What he saw took his breath away.

His grandfather snickered behind him. "It's a sight to behold, isn't it? I love seeing people's reactions the first time they come in here."

Marcus stood still, unable to move, which was a good thing because apparently he was giving his grandfather the appropriate reaction. He'd been briefed on what to expect if he encountered these giant superwolves, but nothing anyone described came close to what he saw below him now. He wasn't even sure he was safe at this distance.

Two dozen wolves covered the floor below. The room was huge, but it paled against the size of those genetically altered beasts. Marcus wondered if their minds were altered as extremely as their bodies, or if they maintained some semblance of themselves under the ridiculous exterior transformation.

The wolves were two and three times larger than normal shifters. Other than their size, they appeared proportionally normal. Marcus had been told they were average-sized when shifted to human form, but he had trouble imagining that currently. "What happened to them?"

"They received gene therapy. My people have

located the specific DNA that controls size and added a chromosome."

"How many are there? Can you do that to anyone?" He knew the answer to the last question was no. Or at least it had been. The real question was whether or not his research was advanced enough to alter those shifters who didn't carry that particular gene. Their latest intel alluded to that possibility.

"Over a hundred now. And not quite yet. But soon." His grandfather slapped him on the back, shocking Marcus with his unexpected gesture. "You want to be the first to give it a try?" He chuckled as though he were kidding.

Marcus didn't believe for a minute the man was kidding. In fact, he'd bet his last day on Earth he'd been brought here for exactly that purpose. "No. Thanks. I think I like myself the way I am." He tried to smile as though he believed his grandfather to be joking. "It doesn't look like that many shifters down there." Marcus peered closer over the edge, pretending to be curious about the numbers.

"They aren't all here on site. Many are at a training facility. The only thing we do here is create them. Once they're declared healthy and released, they go to our other location for training."

"Where is that?" *Please keep the information flowing, Granddad.*

"Virginia, outside Washington D.C."

Marcus twisted his head to see his grandfather. The man stood there with a grin on his face. He was awfully proud of himself.

"Why D.C.?" He knew he wasn't going to like the answer already.

"It's a long story. That's where my benefactor is located. I'll explain more later. Too much information for one day. You look like you're on overload, boy." Melvin patted him on the back. "I'm proud of you for stepping up to the plate and joining the family business."

Marcus turned back to the window. He needed to process everything he'd learned. Benefactor? That couldn't be good. Did it mean someone in the government was in on this scene? Not just a human, but a government official?

Marcus resumed his focus on the supershifters. "What can they do?"

"Fight, of course. And win."

"Fight whom?" *The rest of us shifters? The government?* He fought to keep from shaking.

"Anyone standing in the way of progress."

Marcus wanted to ask what that *progress* was, but he decided to leave that one alone. "What are they doing down there?"

"Sparring. Practicing. Honing their skills."

"Do they shift into human form?"

"Yes. Same as always. They just have extra speed and agility when in their natural form. It's fantastic." The look on the man's face in Marcus's peripheral vision gave Marcus a chill. The man was certifiable. If he'd ever had any doubts, those were laid to rest right that second.

"I see." He didn't, but it seemed like the right response.

They watched in silence for a long time. Marcus decided it was prudent to learn everything he could from these wolves. Their abilities might come in handy at some point. He hoped he could get word out to the reserves in the area what they were up against before they busted into the building, but the option hadn't presented itself.

"Come on. I'll show you more of the facility."

Marcus followed, keeping his gaze on the wolves below as they passed the long window. If they weren't so fucking enormous and crazed, they would look like any other wolves practicing for potential scrimmages in the reserves.

After witnessing that scene, Marcus found very little else in the building to be much of a shock. A tour of the lab showed a dozen shifters working around petri dishes and microscopes. His grandfather explained they were analyzing slices of DNA for potential splicing.

When they came to the end of a row of chairs, Melvin pointed at one and gestured for a man in a lab coat to come over. "Sit," he said to Marcus. "Geoffrey is going to take a vial of your blood."

Marcus stiffened. "What for?" He didn't like the sound of that. At least he seemed to be taking it out, rather than putting something in. That would be much worse.

Melvin patted his arm, placating him. "Just to see if you're a candidate. Always useful to know, right?"

No. Never. If I went my entire life without knowing that,

I'd be fine. But he sat, eyeing the man with the vial suspiciously. *Please God, take blood out. Do not put anything in.* Marcus's main objective for the next eight hours was to keep from being drugged. If he could just make it to the end of the day…

The man named Geoffrey didn't make eye contact or speak a word to Marcus as he efficiently stabbed him in the arm and filled the vial with blood.

"Take it to the lab and test it," his grandfather commanded.

Geoffrey nodded and strode away.

Marcus glanced to his left as he held a cotton ball on the blood welling up under his skin. He hadn't noticed the refrigerator to his side when he'd sat, but now he stared at it, pretending to be preoccupied with his arm. The front door was glass, providing him the opportunity to see its contents. Hundreds of vials of what looked like plasma filled the small refrigerator. Half the vials had Alu47 inscribed on the sides. The other half had Alu79 on them.

Marcus suddenly wished he'd paid closer attention in biology.

"Ready?" his grandfather asked. "Let's get lunch." The man turned to walk away, and Marcus followed, soaking in every detail everywhere they went.

As they sat to eat, his grandfather spoke. "I must say, I'm impressed with your willingness to learn the details of my adventure and join the family."

When he said family, Marcus didn't know if he meant himself or the collective group of shifters in the compound.

"You were ornery as a teenager. Argumentative, I'd say." He took a bite and then continued. "I expected you to be more contentious."

Marcus smiled and shrugged. "Guess meeting my mate changed things. I can't very well support her without a job. What better time than the present to join the family?" He repeated his grandfather's word, leaving it hanging there with no more meaning than it had when Melvin said it. At least in Marcus's mind.

"Well, I'm glad you've come around. You'll be happy with your choice. Trust me."

Marcus thought he should have felt at least the minutest amount of guilt over the fact he was about to throw his grandfather to the wolves, but he couldn't bring himself to feel remorse toward the man who'd made several years of his life a living hell and planned to do God knew what to Marcus now.

He had until six o'clock to gather all the info he could, and then he needed to find a way to get out of this building. The afternoon couldn't pass quick enough.

~

Heather's knees hurt from crouching near the ground all day. She'd slept fitfully in the car during the night. The men had taken turns guarding the cars, watching the compound, and sleeping. Heather hadn't been permitted to leave the vehicle for any reason in the dark.

Now she wished she'd gotten better sleep. She was

exhausted from watching nothing occur at the camouflaged green building she could see through her binoculars. The only signs of life were the four guards roaming the top of the complex. They held semi-automatic rifles and paced the perimeter, trading spots every half hour. Alex explained the building was basically a concrete bunker. Undoubtedly there was someone looking through surveillance cameras at the surrounding area, and unfortunately, gaining entry was probably going to be difficult without taking out the guards on the roof and blowing a hole in one of the entrance doors.

Heather prayed Marcus found a way to get out at six o'clock and he came out the same door he'd entered yesterday. The reserves were watching every possible entrance around the building, but they were best prepared to enter through the east door.

Marcus had fifteen minutes left, and then NAR was moving in with or without him. *Please, God, let him open that door.* She willed him to be okay and able to get out.

They'd chosen six, assuming the inhabitants would be at dinner at that time and Marcus might be able to break free as though heading for the restroom and make a run for it.

It was far-fetched at best, but the only option they'd managed to come up with without communication directly with Marcus since he'd left with his grandfather yesterday.

The chatter between everyone picked up as they readied themselves to move in. They had to go at precisely six because it was what Marcus was expecting either way. If he was trapped inside the compound, he knew at that hour to do his best to find a safe location.

Come on. Come on, Heather chanted inside her head. Alex was staying back with her. The rest were poised to advance. Their numbers increased over the last twenty-four hours from fourteen to a hundred. They had to hope the shock value would play into their plans. With no idea how many shifters were inside the compound, their only guess came from the size of the building.

Heather was holding her breath when Alex's phone vibrated. Even on silent, Heather could hear the distinct low tone.

Alex yanked it from his pocket and pushed talk. He lifted his gaze to Heather. "Hello?"

It was a long shot, but Heather hoped it was Marcus.

And then Alex smiled. "Thank God. Putting you on speaker. I'm with Heather." The phone went from quiet to simmering with possibilities as Alex held it between the two of them. "It's Marcus."

Tears formed in her eyes. She couldn't choke out a hello.

"Hey, baby. Listen, I only have a second. Alex, can you hear me?"

"Loud and clear."

"Postpone your approach until eleven tonight. The majority of the shifters will not only be sleeping, but locked in their rooms." Marcus spoke quickly and quietly. "There are four men on the roof. Take them out and then head for the entrance Melvin and I used when we first arrived. I'll do my best to open the door before you get there. If I'm unsuccessful…"

"We'll blow it open. No worries," Alex said. "What kind of surveillance is there?"

"Cameras everywhere, but I'll do my best to take them out before you approach. As long as you wait until eleven, you should be able to get in and take over the compound virtually unnoticed."

"That would be nice."

"There are about two dozen superwolves in here and maybe two dozen shifters I've only seen in human form. I don't think any of them are enhanced, but I can't be sure. You'll need transportation for that many prisoners and a refrigerated truck."

"Okay. We'll have the appropriate vehicles available."

"Perfect. Gotta go. Eleven. Heather, I love you." Marcus spoke so fast, she didn't have a chance to respond before the line went dead.

She inhaled sharply and wiped her eyes with the back of her hand. She needed to pull it together. Marcus was safe. He would remain that way. He had to.

Alex worked fast to send a group text, informing everyone of the new plan. When he put the phone back in his pocket, he turned to Heather with a smile. "You okay?"

She nodded. "Relieved."

"I bet." He pulled her toward him awkwardly. "I'm not much of a hugger, but you look like you could use one."

She struggled to keep from crying, especially at his sappy sentiment. "You might change your mind when you meet your mate," she said when she found her voice and pulled back.

He gave a short tip of his head to one side. "Perhaps. Not betting on it, though."

Heather rolled her eyes. "Men."

Alex pulled out his phone again. "Jerard says to pull back and regroup."

The two of them inched back from their lookout and met up with several other shifters a few yards from the cars where they'd set up a meeting spot earlier in the day.

Jerard was pacing. "What did he say?" he asked before Heather and Alex reached his side.

Alex recanted the details of the brief conversation, and then Jerard made a few calls to ensure they had enough military transport to transfer fifty people, assuming they managed to take everyone alive.

Once arrangements had been made, there was nothing else to do but wait. The letdown from the anticipated attack weighed on everyone, making them antsy to get the operation under way. But they had no choice but to postpone their attack until Marcus let them in the door or time ran out. To do otherwise would be insanity.

Alex encouraged Heather to lie down in the back of the car for a while, and she took his advice, but sleep wouldn't come. Nerves made her fidgety and restless. Until she had Marcus in her sight, she couldn't relax.

At ten thirty they made their way back to their spots around the compound. It was very dark. Only the dimmest of lights illuminated the sides of the building, probably to keep anyone who happened along from noticing the secret location.

Alex sat on the ground with his legs crossed, eyeing the compound through special night binoculars.

Heather did the same next to him. As shifters, they could see better than any human, even in the dark, but precision was crucial. No one wanted to make an error or miss a signal if anything should change.

"You and I will wait here when the reserves move in."

Heather nodded. She didn't like it, but she couldn't very well run toward combat with no weapon and no training. Alex had been selected as her babysitter because he too had limited military experience. He worked for The Head Council, not NAR.

Jerard wasn't going to be fighting, either. As their leader, his life was more important. And even though he'd been trained in combat in his youth, it had been years since he'd held a gun.

The hardest part was going to be waiting on the outside with no idea what was happening on the inside until someone either called, texted, or came out.

~

Marcus paced in his room, glancing at his watch every few seconds. He should have been exhausted after sleeping only a few hours two nights in a row, but his adrenaline pumped so hard, he couldn't sit.

At ten forty-five, he pushed through the door to his room, relieved to find his plan had worked. It had taken some maneuvering throughout the day to collect everything he needed to plot this revolt against his grandfather and everyone under his command. All he could do was hold his breath and pray the details as he envisioned them went off without a hitch.

At lunch, Marcus had conveniently spilled ketchup all down his shirt. Melvin escorted him back to his room, unlocked the door, and then entered ahead of Marcus. While his grandfather had his back to him, Marcus slapped a piece of duct tape over the hole in the door frame. Step one complete.

Taking a deep breath, he made his way silently down the hall. The tape portion of tonight's entertainment had been his weakest link. With that accomplished, he felt his confidence building. If he hadn't been able to get out of his room, he could have done nothing else.

Memorizing the location of everything in the building had been no small feat, either. He'd spotted cameras in the halls, so he knew there was some level of surveillance, but he hoped the men monitoring the halls at night paid little attention, considering everyone was supposedly locked in their rooms.

His first stop would be security. Marcus had walked by the room several times with his grandfather, and he'd been immensely glad, too, because it gave him the assurance there were always two men on duty, one inside the room and one in the hall. He'd met the man in the hall, Benson, and had spoken to him briefly. He hoped security hadn't increased with the night shift.

Either his grandfather was irrationally confident about his secret location, or the man was a fool. Marcus would bet money on the latter.

The second item Marcus swiped earlier in the day

had been the phone he'd used to call out. That feat had been simple. There were half a dozen flip phones lying in a random corner of Melvin's office, presumably for anyone leaving the compound to use. No one inside the compound had a phone on them. There were internal phones for necessary contact, but undoubtedly good old Granddad didn't want anyone to be able to call out.

With almost no difficulty, Marcus had slid one of those phones off the counter behind him and stuffed it in his pocket while Melvin was making his way behind the desk. Thank God the man moved rather slowly. It had worked in Marcus's favor time and again.

Marcus patted the phone in his pocket once more as he made his way down the dark hall. If all hell broke loose, at least he could call out and warn the others, unless he was incapacitated, or worse. He shook the thought from his head. Dead wasn't an option. Heather would kill him, he thought with a wry grin.

He paused when he came to the last corner, listening closely for the sound of the night guard at the security room. What he encountered instead were voices. Surprise froze him in his tracks. Someone was talking to the guard. Marcus listened closely, flattening himself against the wall.

He didn't recognize the voice, but he held his breath when he heard his own name mentioned.

"Cunningham wants you to keep a close eye on his grandson. He doesn't trust the guy yet."

"He doesn't trust his own grandson?" Benson chuckled.

Marcus sucked in a sharp breath. *What the fuck? Dammit.* He glanced at his watch. *Come on. Come on.*

Benson continued to yap with the unknown man for a few minutes, eating away at Marcus's timeline.

"...'K. I'm turning in for the night. Have a good one," the man finally said.

"You too," replied Benson.

Marcus prayed the man would head in the opposite direction, but no such luck. Footsteps grew closer to Marcus by the second. He had no idea how large the man was or what he was doing up this late at night, and he scrambled to come up with a plan. Attempt to explain why he himself was up? Or fight the guy and try to take him out, alerting Benson to the strife in the hall?

Fuck.

The footsteps grew closer, a nonchalant pace. Marcus righted himself and prayed for a miracle. There was no way he would have the time to fight the man, especially without any notice as to whom he would be up against. He would have to talk his way out of this one.

He guessed he had only a few seconds left as he struggled to come up with an explanation. And then suddenly the man was there, less than two feet from Marcus. He wore green camouflage and was armed for battle. He must have just gotten off a shift outside. But the best part was he had his head dipped down reading something in his hand, and he turned to head down the hallway in a different direction without noticing Marcus.

Marcus didn't move a single muscle as the soldier

ambled down the hall, facing away from Marcus. It took him forever, his pace never increasing. Marcus stared at his back the entire time, thanking God for this small concession in his favor.

Finally, the soldier entered a door on his left and disappeared.

The exhale Marcus released was palpable. He turned his attention toward his goal, wasting no time approaching Benson.

With a deep breath, he put his plan into action, waltzing around the corner as though nothing were out of the ordinary for a man to be out roaming the halls late at night.

"Marcus?" Benson stood from where he'd been sitting outside the security office door. He looked concerned.

"Grandfather sent me to check on things."

Benson rolled his eyes, but then furrowed his brow. Obviously Melvin was highhanded with everyone. It wasn't just Marcus.

The moment Marcus stepped next to the older, dark-haired man, he patted him on the arm. "You know how he can be."

"Don't I ever. He's a good man with excellent intentions and unsurpassed intelligence, but sometimes he definitely overthinks things."

In this case, my friend, he has severely under thought. His negligence in overestimating his grandson's loyalty would cost him everything tonight.

Benson must not have taken to heart what the

soldier had just told him. "You'd better get to your quarters. No one is permitted in the halls at night."

Without hesitating, Marcus leaped at him and wrapped his arm around the older man's neck in a choke hold, squeezing tight until the guard passed out. Marcus eased him to the floor, swiping the keys hanging halfway out of Benson's pocket. He grabbed the gun holstered to Benson's waist next.

Bless him for explaining everything in the security office so thoroughly earlier. All Marcus had had to do was feign interest in the working of their equipment, and the man was a fountain of information, as though no one had ever given him the time of day before that moment.

Marcus unlocked the security room and stepped inside.

"What now, Benson?" Before the guy at the control panel could turn around, assuredly not wanting to exert so much energy and strain his neck away from the riveting surveillance of nothing but the dimly lit night, Marcus cracked the side of his head with Benson's gun. The guy slumped forward, and Marcus caught him fast enough to keep him from falling across the keyboard. He lowered him to the ground and stuck the gun in the back of his own pants.

Working quickly, Marcus dragged Benson into the tiny office and pushed several buttons to disarm the alarm. He glanced at his watch. "Fuck," he muttered under his breath. He was late. He had less than one minute until eleven. There wasn't enough time to run for the door to the outside to open it. Instead he would need to stay low and wait for NAR to blow the entrance. It would alert everyone in the facility, but it couldn't be helped. He just prayed the doors to the individual rooms didn't unlock in the security breach.

Marcus hunkered down in the security office and stared at the monitors. Thirty seconds later he watched as the four soldiers on the roof collapsed in their spots, a precise move that clearly indicated the precision ability of NAR.

Marcus's heart pounded as he waited for what he knew would happen next. Sure enough, an explosion rocked the building. Nothing in the security room was dislodged. NAR used just enough explosives to blow the entrance without taking down the entire building.

Marcus jumped from his crouched position and exited the room to run toward the entrance.

Almost immediately, dozens of camouflaged reserves flooded the hallway.

Marcus motioned for them to join him. He explained the situation as fast as he could while walking toward the living facilities. "With the exception of my grandfather, everyone is locked in their rooms. Obviously they aren't oblivious to the explosion, but I'm confident you can scavenge around and take anything you want during the night and then be prepared to overtake everyone as their doors unlock in the morning."

Marcus stopped walking and pointed down the long hall where all the living facilities were. "A team should ensure my grandfather doesn't escape. Room 100."

Four reserves headed in that direction. It had been

less than a minute. Marcus was relieved to not encounter his grandfather in the hall already. He was also somewhat concerned about that.

"I incapacitated two men in the security office. We need to send some reserves to that room to make sure those guys are taken into captivity before they wake up." Another four reserves headed the direction Marcus indicated.

"In addition, there are about fifty shifters here. The ones in human form have small apartments lined up on the hall I just pointed out. The shifted ones are in another section. They may or may not be in wolf form at the time. But you'll have to be prepared for their strength."

Several reserves nodded.

Marcus led the way deeper into the building, pointing at the highlights of the layout before they divided up to dig into the inner working of the facility.

"This is amazing," one of the reserves whispered to Marcus as he led a group of six into the lab. "I'm Chuck, by the way. I was with the team that rescued Allison Watkins last month. I heard about this place." He nodded at a refrigerator. "We need to take these samples."

Marcus nodded. "And we need to keep them viable. Did you get a refrigerated unit?"

"Yes. I'll have them pull it up to the building." Chuck grabbed his cell from his pocket and sent a quick text. "Done." He leaned in to peer through the glass door. "What the hell do all these numbers mean?"

"Beats me. But I'm sure they're important."

"Alu47, Alu79... They must refer to chromosomes. Don't humans have forty-six chromosomes? And wolves have seventy-eight?" Chuck asked.

"I think so." Marcus cringed as he leaned in. "Wonder what has seventy-nine then, or God forbid, forty-seven."

Chuck stood. "Those superwolves is my guess."

"Fuck." Marcus said a silent prayer, thanking God he hadn't been injected with anything in the day and a half since his arrival. The last thing he wanted was someone fucking with his DNA. He wondered if the superwolves had been converted voluntarily or against their will. Probably some of both, knowing his grandfather. He didn't doubt for one minute the man would have altered Marcus without batting an eye given enough time.

"Look at these three on the bottom." Chuck pointed.

Marcus leaned closer. Alu47/79 was written on them. He stepped back. "Jesus. This is fucked up."

"You ain't kidding," Chuck said. "I feel the urge to step back for fear of contamination from my proximity." He laughed, but unconvincingly.

Marcus righted himself. "I'm going to head for my grandfather's room and make sure he was secured."

Chuck nodded. "We've got this. I think we know everything we need. We'll gather everything we want to take and get it loaded on trucks."

"Do you know where my mate is?" Marcus asked.

"About a quarter mile to the west. She's with Alex, though she isn't happy about it."

"I'm sure. But thanks for keeping her safe."

"Of course. Alex has no business in here, either. He isn't trained in combat."

As Marcus walked away, he continued. "At six o'clock, men need to be stationed in the hall when the doors to the private rooms click to unlock."

Marcus headed for his grandfather's quarters. Four reserves stood inside the room. Melvin wasn't there. Good. Marcus couldn't face the man. Not because he felt any level of remorse for orchestrating this sting, but more because he wasn't sure he could keep from punching him in the face and finally smirking while the asshole got his just reward. "Did you already take him away?"

The men turned toward him. The largest man, a blond, spoke. "He wasn't here."

"Shit." Marcus turned toward the hall and looked in both directions. "How is that possible? He didn't have enough warning to escape. We were here within a minute of the explosion."

"Look at this," one of the reserves said from the back of the room.

Marcus headed deeper into the room to find a trap door in the floor behind the bed. A rug was shoved to the side next to it. "Shit."

The reserve whipped the door open, aiming his rifle down the hole. There was a small light on, but no evidence of anyone in the vicinity. "Luis, you come with me. Maybe we can catch up." The first guy lowered himself down the stairs while the other man leaned over the hole.

Marcus spun around, checking the room to see if

there was any other information he might need while the two reserves took off down the escape route.

The tall blond opened a door on the side of the room. Marcus approached, realizing it was a connector to the room next door. The blond lifted his gun as he crossed the threshold. "It's clear."

Marcus followed him inside. They rummaged around for a few minutes with the other remaining reserves before Marcus picked up a photo of a man with a child. "This is the guy I almost ran into in the hall earlier. He's the one who made me late to open the door for you."

"He must be Cunningham's assistant," the blond said, taking the photo. "Luis and Conrad will catch up to them. They can't have made it too far yet."

A commotion in the hall sent all three of them running for the door. Reserves were screaming as they ran toward the other end of the hall. "Freeze. Hands up."

"Stay back," the blond instructed, holding out a hand to keep Marcus from the fray. "Let NAR handle this."

It wasn't as though Marcus didn't have any training. He was far more capable than most people after yearly summers spent at what he now knew were military camps for the supposedly disenfranchised. Nevertheless, he turned toward his grandfather's room while the other two reserves took off down the hall. After rummaging around in several desk drawers and cabinets in both rooms, he found a semiautomatic in the adjoining room. It would serve him much better than the pistol he'd stuffed in his back pocket after taking out the security guys.

He stepped back into the hall to find several shifters with the Romulus had managed to escape their rooms and were involved in a shootout with the members of NAR. Shit. There must have been an auto-release of some sort in case of invasion. Of course. Melvin wouldn't leave his entire bunker without the ability to defend itself.

Someone screamed as they went down hard. Marcus watched as one of the Romulus hit the ground so hard his head cracked, reverberating through the hall. A reserve stepped over his dead body and continued to pursue the other individuals as they became trapped at the end of the hall.

A vibration in Marcus's pocket made him duck back into his grandfather's room and dig for his phone. He'd only made one call out. If the call coming in were either Heather or Alex, he wanted to know.

Sure enough, the screen indicated the call coming from Alex's phone. Marcus flipped it open. "Hello?"

No one responded. He heard a scream and then a shot. He gripped the phone tighter and held it closer to his ear. "Alex?" He shouted again, "Alex? Heather? Talk to me."

Another scream, this one high-pitched. *Heather*.

Marcus turned and ran, giving only a long enough glance down the hall both ways to ensure he wasn't in any eminent danger. He took off for the main hall and headed for the exit they'd blown in the side of the building.

West, he told himself as he bounded over the debris and bolted for the tree line. He could see flashes of light.

Another gunshot rang out, helping guide him. His heart bounded. *If that bastard kills Heather...* He pulled the pistol from his back pocket as he ran.

When he heard voices, arguing, he slowed to avoid detection. He ducked behind a bush and tried to get a handle on the scene in front of him.

He spotted Heather immediately. His grandfather held her around the neck. She was pleading, her sweet timbre standing out above the men surrounding the clearing. "Please. You don't have to do this." Her voice was hoarse. She held on to Melvin's forearm.

"Listen, bitch, unless you want me to shoot that bastard again, stop squirming and go peacefully."

Heather stared at the ground, freezing in her spot.

Marcus followed her gaze and found Alex on his back. He was moving, one foot pushing against the ground in an effort to get out of the line of fire.

Heather screamed.

"Shoot him," Melvin demanded.

That's when Marcus saw the larger soldier from the hall earlier behind Melvin, his gun aimed at Alex. He didn't hesitate. His shot rang out loud, piercing the air. Marcus watching in horror as Alex rolled at the last second, barely avoiding the shot.

Marcus lined up his pistol and took aim, deciding to go for his grandfather first. He was the immediate threat to Heather. *Please stay still, baby.*

He paused only long enough to ensure Heather wasn't going to get shot. His grandfather snarled. "Fucking kill that bastard," he shouted at the soldier to his left.

The man took aim again.

While Melvin watched, Marcus took his opportunity. He lined up the shot and pulled the trigger.

As though in slow motion, a second shot rang out less than a second after the first. Marcus knew he hadn't fired the shot. He stared at the scene in front of him as Melvin and then his body guard fell to the ground.

Heather screamed and screamed.

Marcus lurched to his feet, glancing behind him to find a reserve two feet away from him, lowering his weapon.

As Marcus jerked his gaze back to Heather, she collapsed to the ground, landing on her knees, grasping her neck.

For a moment, Marcus was sure she'd been hit. And then she removed her hands, and he realized she'd been massaging the spot where Melvin had held her.

He leaped over the bush and ran toward her. "Heather," he shouted.

She jerked her face up, tears streaming down her cheeks.

As Marcus approached, she flinched, landing on her butt, and then she recognized him and relaxed her body as he reached her and pulled her into his arms.

She twisted around to face his grandfather before Marcus could stop her. "Oh, God."

Marcus cupped her cheeks and brought her gaze to his.

"You shot him."

"Yes. It was either him or you. He was going to take you hostage."

She wrapped her arms around him and held on tight.

"You two okay?" The deep voice behind Marcus made him twist his neck to see the reserve. He shrugged. "I saw you take off from the facility like a bat out of hell and followed you."

"Thank you. God, thank you so much." If it hadn't been for him, firing the second shot at his grandfather's guard nearly simultaneously, who knew what might have happened?

Heather released Marcus and pushed to her knees, crawling across the ground before he could stop her. "Alex," she yelled.

The reserve crouched in front of Alex, taking his pulse.

"I'm okay," Alex whispered. "Just a flesh wound." He grinned, clearly for Heather's sake.

Marcus beat her to Alex's side. "You've been shot."

"Just in the leg. I'll live. Thanks to you two." Alex lifted to sitting. "Are you okay, Heather?"

"Yes." She grabbed Marcus's arm and leaned in next to him. "Fine."

"I'm so sorry." Alex turned his gaze to Marcus. "They came at us from behind so fast we couldn't react. One second we were watching the scene unfold through binoculars; the next second I'd been shot in the leg, and Heather was in the grip of that madman. I still can't believe a guy as frail-looking as Cunningham could hold on to Heather like that." He pointed at Marcus's grandfather on the ground. "Did you make sure those bastards were indeed good and dead?"

"I did," said the reserve. "They were both shot in the head." He wrapped a piece of his shirt around Alex's leg as he spoke.

Marcus looked at Alex. "How did you manage to call me?"

"What? I didn't call you."

Marcus whipped out his phone. He stared at the incoming call. "You did. That's when I came running."

Alex reached for his pocket and found it empty. He glanced at the ground, located his phone near him, and lifted the device. "Holy shit. I must have accidentally hit redial as I fell to the ground." Alex yanked his gaze to Marcus. "That was your grandfather."

"In blood only. He was no family of mine." He pulled Heather closer to his body and buried his hand in her hair. "The only family I need is right here." He laid his forehead against hers as he spoke. Relief didn't begin to describe what he felt.

She gripped his shirt and held on tight.

"I need to get back," Marcus stated.

"I'm going with you."

He shook his head. "No way. You're staying with Alex." He hauled her to standing.

Alex spoke next. "Neither of you needs to be inside that building. Wait until you get the all-clear before you approach."

The reserve helped Alex to his feet, and Alex braced himself against the guy's shoulder to hobble behind Marcus and Heather.

They approached the facility slowly while Alex spoke to Jerard on the phone. "I'm fine. Flesh wound…

We're just to the west... Yes... Text me when it's clear to approach... Okay... Yep... Got it."

Marcus stared at him.

"We wait here until Jerard says it's clear."

Marcus fidgeted while they waited inside the tree line. They could see the building clearly beneath the lights NAR had put up around the outside. Shifters were being led out and brought to transport vehicles to be removed from the scene.

Jerard came out finally and waved them closer. "Flesh wound?" He raised his eyebrows at Alex as the four of them approached.

"I'll be fine."

They gathered with Jerard about five yards from where NAR was herding the Romulus into trucks.

Someone screamed. "You bitch!" The man broke free of the escort holding him and stomped toward Marcus's group, fire in his eyes.

Heather gasped, gripping Marcus's arm so hard he couldn't feel the circulation.

"You goddamn whore!" the guy screamed.

"Shit. That's the guy who kidnapped me." She stiffened.

Marcus turned toward her as the guy approached. "You said you never saw him."

"I would never forget his voice." She trembled.

Two reserves grabbed the man by his arms to haul him back toward the truck. He was lucky they didn't shoot first and ask questions later. Marcus assumed they'd already ensured everyone was unarmed.

Marcus peeled Heather's hand off his arm and freed

himself from her grip. "Stay here." His voice didn't sound like himself even to his own ears. He marched forward until he was less than a foot from the asshole who'd kidnapped his mate, drugged her, and held her hostage in a basement for a week.

Without hesitation he swung his fist through the air, breaking the man's nose with a loud crunch. Blood splattered everywhere. Marcus's knuckles hurt like a mother fucker, but he didn't stop there. He ignored the pain and punched the guy in the stomach next.

When the guy buckled forward, the reserves lost their grip on his. He fell to the ground, landing in a ball with his knees drawn up.

Marcus kicked him this time. "You son of a bitch," he screamed.

The reserves grabbed for the man on the ground while Heather tugged on Marcus from behind. "Stop it," she yelled. "It's over. They've got him."

Marcus kicked again.

"Marcus! Stop. That's enough. Let the reserves handle this."

He turned toward his mate, his body tense with anger. "This man kidnapped you," he shouted.

"I know. And I'm right here. I was rescued. Let NAR do their job." She pulled his shirt sleeve until he inched toward her.

Staring into her eyes, he finally let his body loosen and slumped toward her. He buried his face in her hair and wrapped his arms around her middle. "You could have died…or worse."

"I know. But I didn't."

Marcus took deep breaths, breathing in his mate's floral shampoo. She calmed him by degrees as the seconds passed. The shuffling behind him grew distant as the reserves removed the man and carted him away. Marcus could hear the guy whimpering from his injuries. Good. Served him right.

"I'm okay," Heather repeated.

He lifted his gaze from her head and stared into her eyes.

She was smiling at him, her hand soothing his cheek now.

He nodded. "I'm the luckiest bastard alive."

She lifted onto her tiptoes and kissed his lips. "Close. Second luckiest."

∼

Hours later, after Alex had been taken to the hospital, Marcus sat in his grandfather's office rummaging through his papers. Heather sat next to him on one side, Jerard on the other.

It had taken nearly three hours to round up and haul away all the captured members of the Romulus. Only five of the Romulus in human form had been killed.

Many of the superwolves were tranquilized. Others had cowered into submission when they realized the odds they faced. Three wolves were shot in the skirmish, but none of the wounds were life threatening. Marcus knew one of the aspects of the supergene was quicker healing. Those wolves would be as good as new before they reached their new prison.

Marcus looked around, realizing this facility was nothing more than a prison itself. It would take months of careful questioning to determine how many, if not all, of those superwolves had been created and held against their will. No one would be trusted in the time being.

After everyone was cleared out and the entire facility had been combed for stragglers, the transport vehicles left in a caravan headed for Seattle.

"Be aware. I believe the shifters in human form have been drugged to keep them from shifting. As that wears off, who knows what they will do," Marcus told Jerard.

"You did a lot of research in the short time you had here," Jerard said.

"I didn't want to risk anything going wrong. I had a vested interest." He smiled, glancing at his mate.

Two dozen members of NAR remained to continue scouring the place for any evidence to help them piece together the big picture.

Why was the Romulus doing this? It seemed excessive as a means to overthrow The Head Council. And knowing the bulk of their supershifters were in D.C. only made the situation that much more suspicious. Someone had funded this operation. It was certain Melvin Cunningham hadn't come up with the billions in research on his own. The idea someone in Washington, someone undoubtedly human, was behind this, shook Marcus to the core.

Heather glanced around. "What are we doing in here? This place gives me the creeps."

"Digging through Melvin's desk. We'll hack into his

computer later. But I want to comb the entire room for any paperwork that might be useful." Marcus grabbed her hand and pulled her close again. "I love you." He looked her in the eye.

"I love you too." She smiled. "Now let's get this done and get out of here. I've heard a rumor my mate can't hold down a job, and he needs to start applying elsewhere."

Marcus chuckled. "I heard a rumor *my* mate has a nursing degree, and she can get a job anywhere in the country and make me a perfectly content kept man."

Heather swatted at his arm.

Marcus was joking. He'd never do any such thing, but it was good to know they could go anywhere Heather's heart desired as soon as this was over. Marcus had no intention of ever returning to Iowa, and Heather had expressed no interest in going home to Oregon, so they were free to explore any option.

"What's this? It has your name at the top." Heather held up a document and handed it to Marcus. "What's an Alu element?"

"Shit." Marcus shook as he read the report. "Looks like it's the result from the bloodwork the lab took yesterday. He read one sentence aloud. "Marcus Cunningham—excellent candidate for Alu47. He doesn't have the gene marker for Alu79. Further testing needed to confirm Alu47/79."

"What does that mean?"

Marcus's hands shook as he let the page fall onto the desk, as though it were contaminated and might infect him. "I'm not sure. If I had to guess, judging from the past, I'd say I don't have the gene marker that would allow me to become one of these superwolves."

"That makes sense. But what about the rest?"

Marcus gritted his teeth. He didn't want to put a voice to his suspicion.

Jerard looked up. "It means he can't be converted into a supershifter in wolf form through simple genetic alteration. The forty-seven indicates he could be transformed into a superwolf through alteration of his human DNA with the introduction of a new chromosome. Some of these giant wolves were altered through their human DNA and others through their wolf DNA."

Marcus stared at Jerard. "How did you figure all that out?"

"We've been researching it for weeks. We took blood samples from the hostages we picked up at the ranch last month. It's all a bit Greek to me, but I'm catching on."

No one spoke for several seconds. When Marcus realized Jerard wasn't going to continue, he broke the silence. "What's the last one mean? The forty-seven, seventy-nine?"

"I'm not sure. We didn't have evidence of that one. Until you found those vials in the lab, I hadn't heard of that combination." Jerard shuffled through the pages on the desk, busying himself with searching for something nonexistent.

"But you have a suspicion."

He paused, blew out a breath, and lifted his gaze first

to Heather and then to Marcus. "It's nothing more than that. A suspicion."

"And?"

The head elder held Marcus's gaze. "There are a couple of possibilities. It could be a new drug that would alter shifters in either human or wolf form."

"But you don't believe that." Marcus knew he wasn't going to like the other option.

Jerard's voice lowered. "It could be something entirely different that would convert regular humans into shifters."

Marcus didn't move. He'd known it was what Jerard would say. He just hadn't wanted to voice it out loud himself.

Heather gasped, putting her hand over her heart. "Is that possible?"

Jerard nodded. "After everything I've seen lately, anything is possible if you have enough money."

"Where do you think Melvin was getting the currency to fund this operation?" she asked.

"From someone in the government."

"The human government? As in Washington D.C.?" Marcus feared that since learning the rest of the supershifters trained in D.C.

Jerard nodded.

"Do you think we thwarted their efforts? My grandfather said most of the superwolves are at a training facility outside D.C."

"Not surprising. We certainly didn't pick all of them up today. More than that were captured at the Spencer ranch in Texas. I believe Cunningham upped the rate of transformations in the last weeks. The ones we picked up here today were probably newly converted."

"So the shifters working in the lab had undoubtedly been kept in a drugged state that prevented them from shifting while they were used as work horses."

Jerard nodded. "Many were rogue wolves he lured in with promises of a better life."

"My grandfather is dead now. Maybe there's a way to locate this training facility and put an end to all this mayhem."

"I wouldn't count on it." Jerard shook his head. "I'm afraid this operation is much larger than we can imagine. I doubt Melvin's death will be more than a blip on the radar."

"What about the women you rescued?" Heather asked. "I didn't see any female supershifters anywhere. What was the purpose of our kidnapping and what drugs were we given?"

"It seems the drugs were various combinations of Rohypnol and scopolamine. I believe you were given the shots to keep you malleable and docile while they tested you for other indicators. Those drugs are like date rape drugs. They probably intended to trick you into believing someone was your mate." Jerard pulled a chair out from under the desk and sat.

Marcus remained standing. "Those date drugs you mentioned are probably the ones I was given last year."

Jerard nodded. "Undoubtedly. That would have been in the early stages of Melvin's research. He used you as a guinea pig to determine how far he could take the level of suggestion."

"It didn't work."

"Ah, but it did. You believed both Kenzie and then Kathleen Davis were your legitimate mates. The only fault was they hadn't received the same drug. Perhaps Melvin didn't care about the failure of the test. He might have considered it a success that you made the attempt to mate them."

Marcus shivered. Jerard was correct.

Heather wrapped an arm around Marcus, setting her head on his shoulder. "So what do you think he intended to do with the women, including me?"

Jerard shifted his gaze from Marcus to Heather. "I'm sure Cunningham intended to create a new army from birth. He was probably on the cusp of altering DNA either before or during gestation."

She squeezed Marcus's arm tighter. "Breeding? To make more superwolves?"

Jerard nodded. "Reproduction. Yes. I think he was selecting males who had the indicator in their genetic makeup and intending to breed them with the hopes of creating an entire new species of superwolves from conception."

"I didn't have the right genes, did I?"

Marcus turned to Heather, confused. "How do you know that?"

"Because I didn't have a microchip in me. I wasn't as valuable."

"Bingo." Jerard smiled.

Heather gave a sharp inhale. "That means Daniel Spencer's mate, Allison, did have the right gene."

"Yes. That's why she's under protection. We didn't

want to take the risk she or any of the other six women that had a GPS tracker in them were kidnapped again."

"Do you think they're safe now?"

Jerard shook his head. "To be honest, I'm not sure how much good it will do to have made this raid and shut down this operation. We can hope, but the reality is there are other superwolves out there already. Even if we rounded them all up, I don't think this madness would stop. The infrastructure of the Romulus is deep. So many people work under Cunningham, I can't guess the number.

"I'd like to think by cutting off the head, we've put a stop to this madness, but if someone in Washington is bankrolling the operation, there's no telling how easy it would be to open up another facility under different leadership tomorrow. They most likely have all the same data we stole." Jerard shook his head in dismay. "I'm afraid this is war, the likes of which our species has never undergone. And the end to our lives under the radar.

"I'll be heading back to Seattle now to meet with everyone in The Head Council office. Now that we know who the mole was, we no longer need to tiptoe around. Everyone needs to be informed. Everyone needs to prepare. Including all civilian shifters. We're going to have to mobilize fast to ensure the maximum number of shifters knows what's coming."

Marcus hated every word he was hearing, but he had to agree. Even if his grandfather was just the catalyst who got the ball rolling, the likelihood his demise would put an end to the threat was slim. Another leader could be elevated to the head position in a heartbeat. Another compound could open anywhere in the world.

In fact, it probably already had…

"We've met at the Gatherings for almost one hundred years. Tonight we must accept *that* time has come to an end. We must prepare for a new way of life, one in which we find a way to live in harmony with humans and help them fight against the evil that's coming." Jerard stood. "Let's get back to Seattle."

Marcus swallowed. Seattle wasn't the first place he'd intended to head when this was over. It hadn't made the short list.

Jerard glanced at them both. "If you don't mind, I'd like you two to accompany me. You were instrumental in shutting this facility down. Many people will have questions about the last few days, hell…years, you both endured, especially you, Marcus. If you're in agreement, I'd like to bring you onto my staff."

The older man turned toward Heather. "You too, Heather. We're going to need medical personal. Lots of them. You'll need to be brought up to date about the latest genetic research, of course, but we'll be floundering to get on top of this and every doctor and nurse available will be crucial to our operation."

Heather nodded. "I'll do anything I can." She lifted her face to Marcus.

Lord, she was amazing. He loved her more now than ever before. "Wherever you go, I go. Seattle it is."

EPILOGUE

ONE MONTH LATER...

Marcus looked at the caller ID on his phone, not recognizing the number or area code. He glanced at his watch. Jerard was expecting him to attend a meeting in five minutes. On impulse he took the call. "Peters speaking." He smiled to himself. He'd gone against the grain of society and taken his mate's name. He never wanted to be associated with the name Cunningham again in his life.

"Hello. Is this the office of Ralph Jerard?" The deep, sure voice was not one Marcus recognized.

"It is. How may I help you? This is his assistant." Marcus stood, tucking the phone under his chin and grabbing a stack of file folders as he gathered items for the meeting.

"This is Secretary of Defense, William Bradford. I was hoping to make an appointment with Mr. Jerard at his earliest convenience."

Marcus froze, dropping the files back on his desk

and gripping the phone tighter with his hand. *The Secretary of Defense?*

"Um." He was speechless. What did Mr. Bradford want with Jerard?

"It's a matter of national security and essential I speak with him as soon as possible," Mr. Bradford continued.

"Of course, sir. I'm sure Mr. Jerard would be interested in speaking with you also. Is this a good number for you? I'll check with him and get back with you within the hour."

"Yes. This is my private cell. It's secure. Is this a good number to contact Mr. Jerard?"

"Yes, sir. I'm his personal assistant. I'm available twenty-four/seven."

"Good. I'm sure Mr. Jerard is a busy man, but I hope you can arrange something for me, preferably without informing anyone else and on neutral territory. I'm in Seattle now. Name the time and the place, and I'll be there."

"Yes, sir. I'll get back with you right away, sir."

"Thank you, Mr. Peters. I appreciate your help." The line went dead.

Marcus's hands shook. *This could be the break we've been waiting for.* Hastily he left the room, abandoning his files altogether and striding quickly down the halls of The Head Council's office building. When he rounded the door to the conference room, he found half a dozen people already gathered.

Jerard had his head bent over some document,

looking at the details with the woman next to him. His reading glasses were perched on his nose.

Marcus silently approached and bent to whisper in his boss's ear. "Something urgent has come up. Can you postpone this meeting?"

Jerard lifted his gaze, his brow furrowed. He must have read the seriousness on Marcus's face, however, because he immediately curbed his surprise and turned to the room at large. "I'm sorry, everyone. Something's come up. We need to postpone until later today." He stood and turned toward Marcus. "What time shall I say?"

Marcus shook his head. "You won't be available today at all." He pursed his lips.

"All right, then. I'll email you all later with a new meeting day and time. My apologies." He nodded at everyone and followed Marcus from the room.

Marcus felt an overwhelming sense of loyalty toward his new boss of a month. And clearly the man trusted him enough to rearrange his world on a dime if that's what Marcus deemed necessary. No questions asked.

Jerard's previous assistant, Alex Marshall, had been elevated to a new position within The Head Council. According to Jerard, selecting Marcus as his replacement had been an easy choice.

Never had Marcus approached Jerard with a request as this one this morning, and he felt relieved he hadn't needed to expound on his request in front of everyone in the room.

Without a word, Jerard followed Marcus down the hall and out a side door.

Marcus didn't utter a single syllable until they stood halfway across the outdoor patio area, typically used by employees taking a lunch break or needing a moment of privacy. This constituted the single most necessary need for privacy Marcus had encountered since Jerard hired him.

Jerard waited.

Marcus glanced around to ensure himself they were indeed alone. "I just got a call from William Bradford, Secretary of Defense."

Jerard gasped.

"He wants to meet with you ASAP. I told him I would call him back as quickly as possible."

"Wonderful. Hopefully this is the break we've been waiting for."

"How can we be sure he knows anything?"

"We can't. But we can hope. If we don't find a champion on our side within the U.S. government soon, we're doomed to failure. God knows what the Romulus has planned in D.C., or anyplace in the world for that matter."

"Well, he sounded serious and made it perfectly clear it was urgent. I have to assume he came to Seattle for this reason alone."

"So, he's here? In Seattle?"

Marcus nodded.

"Well, what are we waiting for? Call him back. Let's go meet him."

∼

It was late, after nine o'clock, when Marcus finally came through the front door of the apartment he shared with Heather. They'd moved into the housing base at NAR when they'd come to Seattle. They weren't the only civilians living and working in close proximity to The Head Council. Living on base had been a no-brainer. It was the only location where their safety could be assured.

Heather stepped into the living room from the kitchen, a smile on her face. "Long day?" She came straight to him as he dropped his briefcase on the floor next to the door and kicked off his shoes. She did this every night without fail, and it warmed Marcus's heart to know she waited eagerly for him. He certainly entered the apartment eager for her each evening.

His mate wrapped her arms around his chest and kissed him until he softened beneath her, his heart rate slowing, his breathing easier.

"Interesting day," Marcus said as she released his lips. "The Secretary of Defense called me, and I took Jerard to meet with him." Most normal employees of any governing force wouldn't share such intimate details with their spouses, but there was nothing normal about Heather's involvement in this operation, and Marcus was glad. If he had to keep hundreds of secrets from Heather, it would have driven him bonkers.

Heather raised an eyebrow and tugged Marcus to the couch. She pressed him to sit and then straddled his lap, pressing her pussy against his cock. This wasn't unusual for her, either. She went to work on his tie as she questioned him. "Wow. That's huge. What did he want?"

"Apparently he's been spying on the Secretary of Homeland Security, Mr. George Fitzsimmons, and gathering intel for quite some time. He'd grown suspicious when large sums of money were being allocated to a mysterious recipient. It would seem the Secretary of Homeland Security is our government mole. Mr. Bradford finally had enough information to definitively discover the existence of shifters."

Heather dropped the tie she'd removed and met Marcus's gaze. "Are you shitting me?"

Marcus shook his head. "I wish. But this is a good thing. We already knew there had to be some humans out there aware of our existence. We knew the funds had to be coming from somewhere in the government. At least now we've met with a man who's on our side in this mess."

"He said that?"

"Yes. He's been snooping around for months. He knew more about The Head Council than I do. He was beyond informed and ready to make us a deal."

"What deal?" Heather went to work on Marcus's shirt buttons.

"My grandfather's people are so organized, there's no stopping them. Even with Melvin gone, we can't prevent the wheels that were already in motion. Apparently Mr. Fitzsimmons thinks he has himself an army of supershifters to use at his disposal."

"And what does he think he's going to use them for?"

"To overthrow the government for starters."

Heather gasped. She released Marcus's open shirt and grabbed both sides in her fists. "Do you think that's possible?"

"It was a lot more likely before today. But now we have Bradford on our side. And he has us on his. He's willing to do anything to keep the government from falling to this bunch of assholes, of course. There may be almost a hundred supershifters at large ready to go to war, but they can't compare to the numbers we have in the North American Reserves, especially if you toss in the United States military."

Heather nodded, her shoulders lowering as her heart rate slowed. "That's a good thing."

"It's a great thing." Marcus tucked his hands under her ass and squeezed. "Jerard is flying to D.C. with Mr. Bradford as we speak. He'll meet with a constituent from the government that's coming together to work with NAR. They'll hold off leaking any information about shifters to the general public, or even the rest of the government, until there's no other choice. If the Romulus pushes them against a wall, NAR will come out. Until then, let's hope the group in D.C. can help contain this problem.

"It's the break we've been waiting for. Instead of having to pick someone inside the cabinet and hope for the best explaining our species and our issues, the government has come to us. Melvin Cunningham's band of rogue superfighters is going down." Marcus kissed her lips firmly. "This calls for a celebration."

"What did you have in mind?" Heather tipped her head to one side and smiled at him coyly. She ran her palms over his bare chest and pushed his shirt off his shoulders. The imp pressed her pussy firmly against his hardening cock.

Marcus lifted himself off the couch, forcing Heather to wrap her legs firmly around his waist as she squealed. He headed down the hall to their bedroom and didn't pause until he had her flat on her back, his body hovering over hers. "Take your clothes off, baby."

Heather scrambled to pull her shirt over her head. She dropped it on the bed and then squirmed out of her skirt. Her bra and panties followed.

Marcus smiled at her. God she was sexy. Marcus tipped his head back, closed his eyes, and inhaled her scent deeply. When he lowered his gaze to her, he grinned. "I see."

"You see what?"

"The reason why you're so horny today."

"Can't a woman simply be horny without a specific reason?"

Marcus unbuttoned his pants and then shrugged them over his hips, taking his underwear with them. He pulled off his socks and climbed up between his mate's spread legs. "Sure they can. Or they can be in heat."

Heather sucked in a breath. She squirmed backward away from Marcus's approach. "Are you serious?"

"Yes." He grabbed her legs and pulled her back toward him until her pussy lined up with his cock. The damn hard-on he had was worse than ever, compliments of his mate's pheromones. "But don't look so concerned. I told you I would never intentionally impregnate you until you were ready." He leaned over her and took a nipple between his lips, sucking until she writhed and grabbed his biceps.

When he popped off, she spoke again, her voice ragged with arousal. "Now isn't a good time, Marcus. The world is too uncertain."

"I agree." He sucked her other nipple into his mouth next.

She firmed her grip. "Then what are we going to do?"

Marcus finally took pity on her. He lifted his head from her chest and leaned over to the bedside table to extract a condom. When he returned to center, he held it up. "I hate these things."

"Me too. But…"

"I know." He smiled. "No worries. I'll protect you from my swimmers for a few days." As much as he would love to have a child with Heather, he had to agree with her reasoning. Now was a bad time. Hopefully soon the world would be a better place, and they wouldn't have to worry about so many factors concerning the birth of another shifter. He ripped the foil open and rolled the condom onto his cock.

"Thank you." She visibly relaxed her frame.

He stroked a hand between her breasts, across her stomach, and lower. When he pressed into her pussy, he found her wetter than ever.

Heather moaned and lifted her torso into his touch.

Marcus set one hand on her torso and pressed her firmly into the mattress. He needed her as badly as she did him. The urgency had skyrocketed with her ovulation. He couldn't bring himself to tease her tonight as he normally did. Instead, he swiped his fingers through her folds and across her clit. "So wet, baby."

Heather didn't respond. Her eyes glazed over as she watched him.

He didn't wait another moment. Taking her by surprise, he leaned over her, straddling her with his elbows on both sides of her head, and thrust into her.

She screamed.

He never took her that fast. He usually enjoyed the game they played where he tortured her with his fingers and his lips until she pleaded with him to let her come.

Tonight was different, however. Tonight he had renewed hope for the world. Tonight Heather's scent drove him quickly to the edge. Tonight he needed to be inside her immediately, reassured by her pussy gripping his cock that life was good. The world was still a good place. They would survive.

Marcus thrust harder. He dipped his hands under her knees to press them up and away from her body. It gave him the deepest penetration.

Heather moaned. Her head rolled back and forth. She grabbed his biceps tighter.

"Marcus. I'm going to come."

He nibbled a path to her ear and whispered, "Come with me, Heather. Now."

They both crashed over the edge at the same moment, an orgasm that took Marcus's breath away even with the addition of the condom.

He kissed his mate thoroughly, delving into her

mouth with his tongue as the pulses of her orgasm slowed.

"I love you. We're going to be okay."

"I love you too," she mumbled against his mouth.

Marcus stared into his mate's eyes for long moments, hoping his optimism was well-founded. He prayed the two sides of this impending war could work things out with minimal loss of life.

He looked forward to a long and happy future with his mate. They were just starting out. They deserved the same life expectancy generations of shifters before them had experienced.

It had to work. He would accept no other option.

AUTHOR'S NOTE

I hope you've enjoyed this last book in the Wolf Gatherings series. Please enjoy the following excerpt from the first book in the Arcadian Bears series, *Grizzly Mountain*.

GRIZZLY MOUNTAIN

ARCADIAN BEARS, BOOK ONE

Isaiah Arthur leaned against the side of the brand new, dark blue Honda Accord, holding a woman's jacket to his nose. He didn't need the proximity to her clothing to catch and memorize her scent. The open car door was sufficient.

He breathed in deeply again, letting his eyes close briefly as he inhaled her essence. Clean. Feminine. A hint of vanilla, probably from her shampoo. "When did she go missing?" He tried unsuccessfully to shake the lure of her pheromones from his head.

The woman was lost. He had a job to do. Find her. She might not even be alive, and his cock was stiff from leaning into her car to grab her jacket in the first place. One whiff of Heather Simmons and his knees buckled.

"The last time anyone heard from her was yesterday morning. I think she has a room at Bear Lodge in Silvertip. She emailed her hiking route to her mother but never checked back in last night. Mrs. Simmons called us about an hour ago." Glen Montrose, of the

Parks Canada Warden Service, ran a hand through his thick dark hair, his face grim.

Isaiah lowered the jacket, tossing it back into the car reluctantly. "At least we're dealing with a smart hiker this time." It was a good sign that she'd informed someone of her intentions and arranged a check-in time. From that little information, he had hope she also had hiked away from her car prepared for the elements.

He glanced at his watch. Eight o'clock. Heather spent the entire night in the mountains somewhere. He had no doubt he would find her, but had she brought enough clothes with her to survive a night in the cold? The temperatures had dipped below freezing last night.

Isaiah closed his eyes and breathed in. The only scent in the area, besides Heather's and Glen's, was wild animals and pine. The only noise was the rustling of the trees and the scamper of small animals.

He glanced around the small gravel parking lot. No other cars had been left overnight in this secluded area where hikers sometimes parked before trekking up the mountain. The gravel area was surrounded by a thick grove of trees, and when Isaiah lifted his head, he had the most glorious view of the mountains to the north. Alberta, Canada, was one of the most beautiful places on earth.

Heather Simmons was up this mountain somewhere.

Isaiah was restless to get moving. The sooner he found the missing hiker, the better her chances of survival. And he prayed she was indeed alive.

This was the thirteenth rescue he'd done for Banff

National Park, and it never got any easier. Nine of the hikers he was asked to locate had been found alive, either lost or injured. Three had not been as fortunate. He said a silent prayer that today would turn his saved tally to a double digit.

Shoving off the side of the car, he rubbed his hands together and faced Glen. "I better get going. It's cold out here." He stated the obvious, but he didn't need any further details. He had what he needed—her scent and the last known time of contact. Nothing else mattered.

It wouldn't take him long to track her. As a bear shifter, his sense of smell was superior to nearly every other shifter known to exist. He could shift quickly, run fast, and track in minutes.

Montrose knew that. It was the reason he'd called Isaiah an hour ago to request his help. They had an arrangement. It worked. Although only a select few people working for the National Parks Service were shifters, they managed to connect with Isaiah's extended family whenever their assistance was needed. It wasn't feasible for a park warden to shift and take off looking for a hiker in the middle of the workday. Eyebrows would rise.

Isaiah's only concern was the location of Heather's intended hike—way too close to the divide between his family, the Arthurs, and the neighboring pack of bear shifters, the Tarbens. The feud between the two packs went back more than a century, and crossing into the other pack's territory was forbidden.

Isaiah personally thought the entire feud was shit, but he wasn't a member of the ruling body, and frankly, he didn't want any part of it. If the two packs wanted to battle over a fucking imaginary line in the mountains, let them duke it out for all he cared, as long as no one asked him to get involved.

The truth was, he had friends in the Tarben family. He knew for a fact several others in his generation did, too. They kept their relationships private to avoid pissing off the elders from either pack, but secret meetings had occurred between members of the two families for decades.

Isaiah had known one of his best friends, Austin Tarben, for half his life. The two of them had met up secretly for fifteen years. They bitched often about the absurdity of their families' feuds.

Shaking the errant thoughts from his head, Isaiah stepped away from the car, closed his eyes to settle his mind, and shifted. In moments he shook off his human form and allowed the transformation to take place. He leaned forward as his hands became paws and his body took on all the qualities of his other half—the grizzly bear. Fur replaced skin, bones lengthened and shortened, his face elongated.

The few humans aware of the existence of the bear species often referred to the process as magic, but Isaiah didn't see it that way. Shifting was simply a trait he possessed, no different from being able to roll his tongue, wiggle his ears, or lift one eyebrow while lowering the other. The members of his pack could transform into bears.

Isaiah glanced back at Glen before bounding away. He could have spoken to the other shifter telepathically, but there was no need. He already knew which direction to head. His ability to scent was as fine-tuned in human form as it was in his grizzly, but he could cover more ground faster with a more direct route as a bear. And he was instantly warmer.

His temperature ran high even in human form, but racing through the trees and climbing over rocks and foliage was far easier and more expedient in his bear form.

How far had Heather managed to get before she got lost or injured yesterday?

Please, God, let me find her alive.

Finding a victim no longer living was never pleasant, but something about this particular woman had his fur standing up. Her scent called to him. Lured him.

He hadn't even seen a picture of her. It wasn't necessary. He would know her by her scent the moment he got close.

ALSO BY BECCA JAMESON

Canyon Springs:

Caleb's Mate

Hunter's Mate

Corked and Tapped:

Volume One: Friday Night

Volume Two: Company Party

Volume Three: The Holidays

Surrender:

Raising Lucy

Teaching Abby

Leaving Roman

Project DEEP:

Reviving Emily

Reviving Trish

Reviving Dade

Reviving Zeke

Reviving Graham

Reviving Bianca

Reviving Olivia

Project DEEP Box Set One

Project DEEP Box Set Two

SEALs in Paradise:

Hot SEAL, Red Wine

Hot SEAL, Australian Nights

Hot SEAL, Cold Feet

Dark Falls:

Dark Nightmares

Club Zodiac:

Training Sasha

Obeying Rowen

Collaring Brooke

Mastering Rayne

Trusting Aaron

Claiming London

Sharing Charlotte

Taming Rex

Tempting Elizabeth

Club Zodiac Box Set One

Club Zodiac Box Set Two

The Art of Kink:

Pose

Paint

Sculpt

Arcadian Bears:

Grizzly Mountain

Grizzly Beginning

Grizzly Secret

Grizzly Promise

Grizzly Survival

Grizzly Perfection

Arcadian Bears Box Set One

Arcadian Bears Box Set Two

Sleeper SEALs:

Saving Zola

Spring Training:

Catching Zia

Catching Lily

Catching Ava

Spring Training Box Set

The Underground series:

Force

Clinch

Guard

Submit

Thrust

Torque

The Underground Box Set One

The Underground Box Set Two

Saving Sofia (Special Forces: Operations Alpha)

Wolf Masters series:

Kara's Wolves

Lindsey's Wolves

Jessica's Wolves

Alyssa's Wolves

Tessa's Wolf

Rebecca's Wolves

Melinda's Wolves

Laurie's Wolves

Amanda's Wolves

Sharon's Wolves

Wolf Masters Box Set One

Wolf Masters Box Set Two

Claiming Her series:

The Rules

The Game

The Prize

Emergence series:

Bound to be Taken

Bound to be Tamed

Bound to be Tested

Bound to be Tempted

Emergence Box Set

The Fight Club series:

Come

Perv

Need

Hers

Want

Lust

The Fight Club Box Set One

The Fight Club Box Set Two

Wolf Gatherings series:

Tarnished

Dominated

Completed

Redeemed

Abandoned

Betrayed

Wolf Gatherings Box Set One

Wolf Gathering Box Set Two

Durham Wolves series:

Rescue in the Smokies

Fire in the Smokies

Freedom in the Smokies

Stand Alone Books:

Blind with Love

Guarding the Truth

Out of the Smoke

Abducting His Mate

Three's a Cruise

Wolf Trinity

Frostbitten

A Princess for Cale/A Princess for Cain

ABOUT THE AUTHOR

Becca Jameson is a USA Today best-selling author of over 100 books. She is well-known for her Wolf Masters series, her Fight Club series, and her Club Zodiac series. She currently lives in Houston, Texas, with her husband and her Goldendoodle. Two grown kids pop in every once in a while too! She is loving this journey and has dabbled in a variety of genres, including paranormal, sports romance, military, and BDSM.

A total night owl, Becca writes late at night, sequestering herself in her office with a glass of red wine and a bar of dark chocolate, her fingers flying across the keyboard as her characters weave their own stories.

During the day--which never starts before ten in the morning!--she can be found jogging, running errands, or reading in her favorite hammock chair!

...*where Alphas dominate*...

Becca's Newsletter Sign-up:
http://beccajameson.com/newsletter-sign-up

Join my Facebook fan group, Becca's Bibliomaniacs,

for the most up-to-date information, random excerpts while I work, giveaways, and fun release parties!

Facebook Fan Group:
https://www.facebook.com/groups/BeccasBibliomaniacs/

Contact Becca:
www.beccajameson.com
beccajameson4@aol.com

- facebook.com/becca.jameson.18
- twitter.com/beccajameson
- instagram.com/becca.jameson
- bookbub.com/authors/becca-jameson
- goodreads.com/beccajameson
- amazon.com/author/beccajameson

Printed in Great Britain
by Amazon